Sawyer could hear the voices of the admin staff around him. "No, put it here. Callie's very particular about paperwork. Put the algorithms up on the walls, in the treatment rooms and outside the patient rooms. Everyone has to follow them to the letter."

So, she was a rules and regulations girl? This was about to get interesting.

He wandered over to the room. Callie was standing in her bra and pants, opening a clean set of regulation pale pink scrubs. Last time he'd worn them they'd been green. Obviously a new addition to the DPA repertoire.

The sight made him catch his breath. It was amazing what could lurk beneath those stuffy blue suits and pointy shoes. The suit was lying in a crumpled heap on the ground, discarded as if it were worthless when it easily clocked in at over a thousand dollars. He could see the label from here. Maybe Miss Hoity-Toity did have some redeeming features after all?

Dear Reader

When I was asked by my editor if I would be interested in writing a duet I was delighted and jumped at the chance. The Center for Disease Control in the US has always fascinated me. I work in public health, and love all the work around infectious diseases and immunisation campaigns. The CDC always features heavily in any plague/outbreak/epidemic films that are made, and I was excited at the prospect of having a story along those lines and set about creating my own fictional organisation, the Disease Prevention Agency, for my *Rebels with a Cause* duet.

But all stories need to have fabulous characters, and I instantly fell in love with my hero in THE MAVERICK DOCTOR AND MISS PRIM—Matt Sawyer, wounded bad boy and very much like his namesake, Sawyer in *Lost*. He's the kind of guy you know deep-down has real good in him. It's just going to take a special woman to unearth it.

My sassy heroine Callie is a girl out of her depth. She takes the initial call at the DPA and assembles the team, but her mentor is taken unwell on a plane and she's left in charge of a situation that is clearly bigger than any she's coped with before.

Her only option is to turn to Sawyer for help. After all, he worked in the DPA previously and has the expertise she needs. So why doesn't he want to help? It makes quarantine very interesting…

Both my characters in this story are grieving. And both deal with their grief in their own way. Needless to say I let them get their happy-ever-after. It just takes a while to get there!

Please feel free to contact me via my website: www.scarlet-wilson.com. I love to hear from readers!

Scarlet

The second story in Scarlet Wilson's *Rebels with a Cause* duet
ABOUT THAT NIGHT…
is also available this month
from Mills & Boon® Medical Romance™

THE
MAVERICK DOCTOR
AND MISS PRIM

BY
SCARLET WILSON

First published in Great Britain 2013
by Mills & Boon, an imprint of Harlequin (UK) Limited.
Harlequin (UK) Limited, Eton House, 18-24 Paradise Road,
Richmond, Surrey TW9 1SR

© Scarlet Wilson 2013

ISBN: 978 0 263 23373 5

Scarlet Wilson wrote her first story aged eight and has never stopped. Her family have fond memories of *Shirley and the Magic Purse*, with its army of mice, all with names beginning with the letter 'M'. An avid reader, Scarlet started with every Enid Blyton book, moved on to the *Chalet School* series, and many years later found Mills & Boon®.

She trained and worked as a nurse and health visitor, and currently works in public health. For her, finding Mills & Boon® Medical Romances™ was a match made in heaven. She is delighted to find herself among the authors she has read for many years.

Scarlet lives on the West Coast of Scotland with her fiancé and their two sons.

Recent titles by the same author:

AN INESCAPABLE TEMPTATION
HER CHRISTMAS EVE DIAMOND
A BOND BETWEEN STRANGERS*
WEST WING TO MATERNITY WING!
THE BOY WHO MADE THEM LOVE AGAIN
IT STARTED WITH A PREGNANCY

*The Most Precious Bundle of All

These books are also available in eBook format from www.millsandboon.co.uk

Dedication

This book is dedicated to my two fabulous and
entrepreneurial brothers-in-law, who have put up with
me for more years than I care to remember.
For Sandy Dickson and Robert Glencross, thank you
for everything that you've done for me and my family
and for taking such good care of my sisters!

CHAPTER ONE

Chicago

"Okay, BEAUTIFUL, WHAT you got for me?" Sawyer leaned across the reception desk as the clerk glared at him.

Miriam cracked her chewing gum. "You've been here too long—you're getting smart-mouthed."

"I've always been smart-mouthed."

"And get a haircut."

He pushed his shaggy light brown hair from his eyes then tossed his head. "The long-haired look is in. Besides—I'm worth it."

The clerk rolled her eyes and picked up three charts. "You can have two sick kids with chicken pox in room six or a forty-three-year-old female with D&V behind curtain two." They lifted their heads in unison as the noise of someone retching behind curtain two filled the air.

He shuddered. "Give me the kids." He grabbed the charts and walked down the corridor. His eyes skimmed the information on the charts. Ben and Jack Keating, aged six and seven, just returned from abroad with chicken pox.

He pushed open the door. Unusually, the lights were dimmed in the room. The two kids—brothers—lay on the beds with a parent at each bedside. Alison, one of the nurses, was taking a temperature. She walked over to him, her pregnancy bump just starting to emerge from her scrub trousers. "Sickest kids I've seen in a while," she murmured.

He gave her a smile, his natural instinct kicking in. "You safe to be in here?"

She sighed. "After three kids of my own it's safe to say I'm immune."

Sawyer crossed the room quickly, leaving the charts at the bottom of the beds. Alison was right. These kids didn't look good. Chicken pox could be a lot more serious than a few itchy spots.

"Hi, I'm Matt Sawyer, one of the docs. I'm going to take a look at Ben and Jack." He extended his hand towards the mother then the father, taking in their exhausted expressions before turning to the sink, washing his hands and donning some gloves.

He walked over to Ben. In the dim light it was difficult to see his face, but it looked as if it was covered in red, bumpy spots. "Hi, Ben, I'm just going to have a little look at you."

The six-year-old barely acknowledged that he'd spoken. He glanced at the cardiac and BP monitor, noting the increased heart rate and low blood pressure. At first touch he could feel the temperature through his gloves. He pressed gently at the sides of Ben's neck. Unsurprisingly his glands were swollen. There were a number of spots visible on Ben's face so he peeled back the cover to reveal only a few angry spots across his chest but a whole host across his forearms.

The first thing that struck him was that all of the spots were at the same stage of development. Not like chicken pox at all—where spots emerged and erupted at different times.

Alarm bells started ringing in his head. *Be methodical.* He heard the old mantra of his mentor echoing around him.

He moved to the bottom of the bed and lifted Ben's foot.

There. The same uniform spots on the soles of his feet. He stretched over, reaching Ben's hand and turning his palm over. Red vesicular spots.

He tasted bile in the back of his throat and glanced across the room to where Alison had switched on her telepathic abilities and had already hung some bags of saline and was running through the IV lines.

"Where were you on vacation?"

The boys' father shook his head. "We weren't on vacation. I was working. We've just come back from three months in Somalia. I work for a commercial water-piping company."

Somalia. The last known place for a natural outbreak of this disease.

"Were any of the locals you came into contact with sick?" There were a million different questions flying around his head but he didn't want to bombard the parents.

Mrs Keating nodded. "We were in the highlands. A lot of them were sick. But we didn't think it was anything too serious. We actually wondered if we'd taken a bug to them—we were the first people they'd come into contact with in years."

His reaction was instinctive. "Step outside, please, Alison."

"What?" The nurse wrinkled her brow.

He raised his voice, lifting his eyes and fixing them

on her, praying she would understand. "Wait outside for me, please, Alison."

The atmosphere was electric. She was an experienced nurse and could read the expression on his face. She dropped the IV lines and headed for the door.

"Is something wrong?" Mr. Keating started to stand.

Sawyer crossed to the other bed. Jack was lying with his back to him. He wasted no time by pulling the white sheet from across Jack's chest and tugging gently on his shoulder to pull him round.

Identical. His face was covered. Red, deep-seated round vesicles. All at the same stage of development, a few covering his chest but mainly on his forearms. He opened Jack's mouth. Inside, his oral mucosa and palate were covered. He checked the soles of his feet and the palms of his hands. More identically formed red spots.

He could feel chills sweeping his body. It couldn't be. *It couldn't be*. This disease had been eradicated in the seventies. No one had seen this disease since then.

Then a little light bulb went off in his head. Hadn't there been a suspected outbreak a few years ago that had turned out to be chicken pox? The very thing that this was presumed to be? He ran the list of other possibilities in his head. He knew them off by heart. Anyone who'd ever worked in the DPA did.

But the more he stared at the spots the more convinced he became that it was none of the alternatives.

"How long since the spots appeared?"

The mother and father exchanged glances. "A few days? They had a rash at first then the spots developed. They've got much worse in the last day. But the boys had been feeling unwell before that—headaches, backaches, vomiting. We just thought they'd picked up a bug."

Sawyer felt as if he was in a bad movie. Why him? Why did this have to happen while he was on duty?

Would someone else recognize this? Realize the potential risks? Or would they just chalk it up to a bad dose of chicken pox and discover the consequences later? He'd put all this behind him. He'd walked away and vowed never to be involved in any of this again. He was in the middle of Chicago—not in some far-off country. Things like this didn't happen here. Or they *shouldn't* happen here.

And right now that was he wanted to do again. To walk out that front door and forget he'd ever seen any of this.

He looked at the long inviting corridor outside. He wasn't a coward. But he didn't want this. He didn't want *any* of this. The kind of thing that sucked you in until it squeezed all the breath from you.

A shadow moved outside the door.

But there was the killer. A pregnant nurse standing outside that door. A nurse who had been working with him and had contact with these children. Could he walk away from her?

He glanced upwards. It was almost as if someone had put her here so he *couldn't* walk away. His conscience would never allow him to do that.

If only he didn't know she was pregnant. If only that little bump hadn't just started to emerge above her scrub trousers. That would make this a whole lot easier.

Then he could walk away.

He took a deep breath and steeled himself. He was a doctor. He had a duty of care. Not just to his colleagues but to these kids.

These very sick kids.

He looked back at the parents. "I need you to think

very carefully—this is very important. Did you fly home?"

They both nodded.

"When, *exactly*, did you first notice the rash on the boys? Before or after you were on the plane?"

The parents looked at each other, screwing up their foreheads and trying to work it out.

A detailed history could wait. He knew enough already. He wasn't part of the DPA any more. This was their job, not his. The notification part he could handle—setting the wheels in motion so the processes could take over.

Isolation. Containment. Diagnosis. Lab tests. Media furore.

In the meantime he had two sick kids to take care of and staff members to worry about. Let the DPA do their job and he could do his.

He pulled his smart phone from his pocket and took a picture of Jack's spots and then Ben's. "Wait here."

Alison jumped as he flung the door open. "What on earth's going on?" She matched his steps as he strode down the corridor to Reception. "Don't you think you can get away with speaking to me like that. I want to know what you think is wrong." He watched her as subconsciously her hands went to her stomach. This day was just about to get a whole lot worse.

"Did you touch them?"

"What?" She wrinkled her nose.

"The spots. Did you touch the children's spots?"

She must have read the fear he was trying to hide behind his eyes. "I think I did." She looked as if she might burst into tears. Then realization dawned. "I think I had gloves on." Her voice grew more determined. "No, I'm *sure* I had gloves on."

"And when you took them off, did you touch any other part of your skin?"

Her face crumpled. "I don't think so. But I can't be sure."

His hands landed on her shoulders and he steered her into the nearest free room. He knocked the water on with his elbows and pulled the hand scrub over, opening up a scrub brush for her. "Scrub as if you were going to Theatre and don't stop until I tell you."

She looked pale, as if she might keel over. But her reactions were automatic, pumping the scrub, covering her hands, wrists and forehands and moving them methodically under the running water.

He watched the clock. One minute. Two minutes. Three minutes. Four.

"Sawyer?"

He nodded. "You can stop now."

"Do you know what it is?" She was drying her hands now.

"I think I do. I'm just praying that I'm wrong. Come with me."

They reached the desk. Miriam had her back to them and was chatting loudly on the phone.

Sawyer leaned across the desk and cut the call.

She spun around. "What are you doing?"

"We're closed."

"What?" Several heads in the surrounding area turned. "You don't have any authority—"

"I do. Get me Dr. Simpson, the chief of staff, on the phone." He turned to face the rest of the staff. "Listen up, folks. As of now, we have a public health emergency. The department needs to close—right now." He pointed at Miriam. "Let Dispatch know not to send us any more patients."

He turned to one of the security staff. "Lock the front doors."

The noise level around him rose.

He put his hand on Alison's arm, pulling her to one side. "I'm sorry, honey, but that isn't chicken pox. I think it's smallpox. And we need to contact the DPA."

Atlanta

Callie Turner stowed her bag in her locker and nodded at a few of her colleagues getting changed. She glanced in the mirror and straightened her skirt, taking a deep breath as she gave herself a nervous smile and pulled at her new haircut—an asymmetric blonde bob.

It was meant to signify a new start—a new beginning for her. It had looked fabulous in the salon yesterday, expertly teased and styled. Today it just looked as if she was halfway through a haircut. This would take a bit of getting used to.

First day at the DPA.

Well, not really. An internship and then a three-year specialist residency training program completed within the DPA. All to be part of the Disease Prevention Agency. Eleven years in total of blood, sweat and lots of tears.

All to fulfil someone else's dreams. All to pay homage to someone else's destiny.

Today was the first day of the rest of her life.

She pushed open the door to the telephone hub. "Hi, Maisey."

The short curly-haired woman looked up. "Woo-hoo! Well, look who picked the lucky bag on her first day on the job." She rolled her eyes at Callie. "Go on, then. Who did you upset?"

Callie laughed and pulled out the chair next to Maisey. "No one that I know of. This was just my first shift on the rota." She looked around. "It's kind of empty in here. Where is everyone?"

Maisey gave her a sympathetic glance. "You should have been here two hours ago. They're assembling a team next door. We've got a suspected outbreak of ebola."

Callie's eyes widened. First day on the job and she was assigned to the phones. The crazy calls. While next door the disease detectives were preparing to investigate an outbreak. She bit her lip. "Who took the call?"

Maisey smiled again. "Donovan."

Callie sighed. Typical. The person who took the call usually got to assemble and lead the team. Donovan had a knack of being in the right place at the right time.

Unlike her.

She stared at the wall ahead of her. Someone had stuck a sign up: "NORMAL PEOPLE DON'T PHONE THE DPA."

Never a truer word was said. The phone next to her started ringing. She bent forward and automatically picked it up. It would be a long day.

Four hours later she'd spoken to three health officials, crazy bat lady—who phoned every day—two over-anxious school teachers, five members of the public, and two teenagers who'd obviously been dared by their friends to ring up. Right now all she could think about was a large cappuccino and a banana and toffee muffin.

Her stomach grumbled loudly as she lifted the phone when it rang again. "DPA, Callie Turner, can I help you?"

"This is Matt Sawyer at Chicago General. I've got two kids with suspected smallpox."

She sat up instantly as her brain scrambled to make sense of the words. All thoughts of the muffin vanishing instantly. This had to be a joke. But the voice didn't sound like that of a teenager, it sounded like an adult.

"Well, aren't you going to say anything?" He sounded angry. Patience obviously wasn't his strong point.

She took a deep breath. "Smallpox has been eradicated. It's no longer a naturally occurring disease, Mr. Sawyer."

"Listen, honey, you can call me Doctor. Dr. Matt Sawyer. Ringing any bells yet?"

She frowned. Matt Sawyer? The name seemed familiar. Who was he? And why was he speaking to her like that? She put her hand over the receiver and hissed at Maisey. "Hey, who's Matt Sawyer?"

Maisey's eyes widened instantly, the disbelief on her face obvious. She skidded her wheeled chair across the room next to Callie. "You're joking, right?"

Callie shook her head and pointed to the phone.

Maisey bent forward and pulled the phone away from her ear, replacing it with her mouth. "Outbreak, dead pregnant wife, disappeared off the map."

The pieces of the puzzle started to fall into place and become vaguely familiar. Of course. She *had* heard of this guy. In fact, everyone in the DPA had heard of this guy. He was like a dark, looming legend. But it had been way before her time.

Her training and natural instincts kicked in. There was a protocol for this. She pushed her chair under the desk and pulled up a screen on her computer. "Hi, Dr. Sawyer. Let's go through this."

The algorithm had appeared in front of her, telling

her exactly what questions to ask, why and when. She started to take some notes.

"You said you're at Chicago General. Whereabouts in the hospital are you?"

She could almost hear him sigh. "The ER."

"What are the symptoms?"

"Two kids, returned from Somalia a few days ago. Ages six and seven. Very sick. Febrile, uniform red spots mainly on their faces, forearms, palms and soles. A few on their trunks. Low blood pressure, tachycardic, swollen glands."

She was typing furiously. Somalia. The last known place to have a natural outbreak of smallpox. It did seem coincidental.

But there were a whole host of other diseases this could be. She started to speak. "Dr. Sawyer, have you considered chicken pox, herpes, scabies, impetigo—"

"Stop it."

"What?"

"I know you're reading from the list. I've considered all those things. It's none of them. Check your emails." He sounded exasperated with her.

"What do you mean?"

"Lady, do I have to tell you everything twice? Check your emails. I just sent you some photos. Have you ever seen spots like that?"

She clicked out of the algorithm and into her emails. Sure enough, there it was. Everyone in the DPA had a generic email address starting with their full name. He was obviously familiar enough with the system to know that. There was no message. She opened the attached photos.

Wow.

The phone was still at her ear and she moved her

face closer to the screen to examine the red spots. No. She hadn't seen anything like that before—except in a textbook.

"Show the photo to Callum Ferguson," the low voice growled in her ear.

Callum Ferguson. The only person in their team who'd actually been through the last smallpox outbreak. The only person who'd seen the spots for real. Only someone who'd worked here would know something like that. This phone call was definitely no hoax.

"Give me two minutes." She crossed the room in big strides, throwing open the door to the briefing room where the ebola team was assembling.

"Callum, I need you to take a look at something urgently."

"Kind of busy in here, Callie." The large Scotsman looked up from the floor, where he was packing things into a backpack. Callum was well past retirement age but nothing seemed to slow him down, and his age and experience made him invaluable on the outbreak team.

She lowered her voice, trying to avoid the glare coming across the room from Donovan.

"It's Matt Sawyer on the phone. He needs you to look at something."

Callum looked as though he'd just seen a ghost. His hands froze above his pack. He started to stutter, "Wh-what?"

She nodded and he stood up wordlessly and followed her out of the room.

In the few seconds she had been away from her seat, everything had changed. Her boss, Evan Hunter, was standing in front of her computer, staring at her screen, his two deputies and Maisey at his side. The phone receiver was still lying on the desk.

No one spoke. They just moved out of Callum's way as he reached the screen. His heavy frame dropped into Callie's chair and he glided under her desk.

"Well?"

Evan Hunter wasn't renowned for wasting time. The scowl on his face was fierce and made Callie raise her eyebrows. Hadn't someone told her there had been no love lost between him and Matt Sawyer in the past?

Callum, normally red faced, looked pale. He turned to Evan Hunter and nodded. "I'm sure. I never thought I'd see this again," he whispered.

Everything around them erupted.

Evan pressed his hand on Callum's shoulder. "You're off the ebola team. This is yours—it couldn't possibly be anyone else's, seeing as Matt Sawyer is involved. You're the only one who's ever managed to assert any control over that loose cannon. I want you all over him. Pick your team." He looked at his watch. "It'll take ninety minutes to fly to Chicago. I want you packed and ready to go inside four hours."

He turned and swept out the room, his deputies scurrying after him. Callie was shaken. Had this really just happened?

Callum's voice continued in low tones on the phone. He wasn't even looking at the algorithm she'd pulled up on the screen. His eyes were still fixed on the photo.

"You're sure there's no possibility that this could be intentional—a biological terrorist attack?" He was scribbling notes as he listened. There were a few more mumbled questions before he replaced the receiver.

"Was it him? Was it definitely Sawyer?" Maisey looked fit to burst.

Callum nodded. "It was him." He stood up slowly, obviously still in thought. "I guess that means he's all right, then." He touched Callie's arm. "Get ready, Dr. Turner. This could be the experience of a lifetime."

"I'm on the team?" She could barely contain her excitement. It was only made slightly better by the look of disgust on Donovan's face over the other side of the room.

Callum smiled at her. "You know the rules, Callie. You took the call—of course you're on the team."

"I'll be ready in half an hour. Let me get the updated plans." She rushed off, her heart thumping in her chest.

First official day on the job and she was on the outbreak team investigating an apparently eradicated disease. Isabel would have loved this.

Callie shoved her bag in the overhead locker and sat down next to Callum. Everything was happening so fast. She hadn't even had time to think.

The doors of the plane were already closed and they were starting to taxi down the runway. The cabin crew was already in their seats—the safety announcement forgotten. The normal rules of aviation didn't seem to apply today.

This was the biggest team she'd ever been part of. There had to be around thirty people on this plane. Other doctors, epidemiologists, case interviewers, contact tracers, admin personnel and, most worrying, security.

Callum had the biggest pile of paperwork she'd ever seen. He was checking things off the list. "Vaccines— check. Protocols—check. N95 filtered masks—check. Symptom list—check. Algorithm—check. Three-hundred-page outbreak plan…" his thumb flicked the edges of the thick document "…check."

He leaned back in his seat. "And that's just the beginning." A few minutes later they felt the plane lift off. Ninety minutes until they reached their destination.

"What have you done about containment plans?"

He nodded at her question. "I've identified a suitable building for a Type-C containment. Arrangements are currently being made to prepare it. In the meantime we've instructed Chicago General to switch their air-conditioning off. We don't want to risk the spread of the droplets. They don't even have suitable masks right now—only the paper ones, which are practically useless."

He shook his head. "Those spots were starting to erupt. These kids are at the most infectious stage of this disease."

Callie shuddered. A potentially deadly disease in an E.R. department. Her mind boggled.

It didn't matter that she was a completely rational person. It didn't matter that she specialized in infectious diseases. There was still that tiny human part in her that wanted to panic.

That wanted to run in the other direction.

The strange thing was that there were colleagues at the DPA who would kill to be in her shoes right now. Her very tight, uncomfortable shoes. Why hadn't she changed them before they'd left? Who knew how long she would be on her feet?

She hesitated. "Who are you relaying the instructions to right now?"

His eyes fixed on the papers in front of him. He didn't look so good. "The chief of staff at Chicago General is Max Simpson. He's following our instructions to the letter. Or rather Matt Sawyer is following our instructions to the letter. He's the only one with any experience down there."

There were small beads of sweat on his brow. He reached into his top pocket and pulled out some antacids.

"You okay?"

He nodded as he opened the packet and popped three in his mouth.

Callum was the calmest, most knowledgeable doctor she'd ever worked with. She'd worked side by side with him through lots of outbreaks. She couldn't ask for a better mentor. But even he looked a little scared. Maybe it wasn't just her after all?

Or maybe it was something else entirely.

She lowered her voice. "He was your protégé, wasn't he?"

"My what?"

"Matt Sawyer. I heard he was your protégé."

Callum grimaced and shook his head. "Do me a favor. Don't let Sawyer hear you call him that. That would tip him over the edge that I presume he's currently dangling on."

"What do you mean?" During all the frantic preparations Callie hadn't had any time to find out more about Matt Sawyer. Only a few whispers and hurried conversations here and there.

This was her first real mission. She'd been out as a danger detective before—when she'd been completing her specialist residency training. But this was her first real chance to prove herself. To prove that she was a worthy member of the team. To prove to them—and herself—that she deserved to be there.

It didn't sound promising if the doctor who'd made the initial call was unstable.

She looked at the pile of papers on Callum's lap. The outbreak plans, the containment plans, the paperwork to use for contact tracing, the algorithms. A plan for everything. A piece of paper for every eventuality. Just the way she liked it. Just the way she'd learned to function best.

Rules and regulations were her backbone. The thing that kept her focused. The thing that kept everyone safe.

Callum followed her gaze. "This could get messy."

"What do you mean? With the disease? The casualties?" She hadn't even stopped to think about that yet. She still had her public health head on, the one that looked at the big picture. She hadn't even started to consider the individuals.

Callum looked kind of sad. "No." He gave a little grimace again. "With Sawyer."

"Sawyer? Aren't you happy to see him again?" She was confused. Hadn't they been friends?

"Under any other set of circumstances I would be. But not here. Not like this. This will be his worst nightmare. Sawyer walked away from all this. The last thing he wants to do is be involved in another outbreak. I can't imagine how he's feeling."

"He's a doctor. He has responsibilities. He has a job to do." She made it all sound so straightforward. Because in her head that was the way it should be.

He sighed. "Things change, Callie. Life gets in the way. Sawyer doesn't live by anybody's rules but his own. He didn't even follow protocol today. He should have notified the state department first but he didn't. He just called the DPA. He called *you*." He emphasized the word as he placed a hand on his chest.

She'd missed that. Miss Rules and Regulations had missed that. In her shock at the nature of the call it hadn't even occurred to her that Sawyer should have contacted the state department first and *they* should have contacted the DPA.

How could she have missed that?

She didn't need anyone to remind her that things could change—that life, or lack of it—could get in the way. She was living proof of that.

Seeds of doubt started to creep into her mind. She'd missed the first rule of notification. And if she'd missed that, what else would she miss? Should she even be on this team?

Rules were there for a reason. Rules were there to be followed. Rules were there for everyone's safety.

Then it really hit her. What was happening before her very eyes.

The last thing she needed to do right now was look at the wider picture. She needed to concentrate on the picture right before her.

Callum was turning gray, with the slightest blue tinge around his lips. His skin was waxy and he was still sweating. His hand remained firmly on his chest.

"Callum? Are you okay?" She unfastened her seat belt and stood up, signaling to some of the other members of the team. "That's not heartburn, is it?"

He shook his head as she started barking out orders to the rest of the team. "Get me some oxygen. Find out how soon till we get there. Can we get an earlier landing slot? Speak to the pilot—it's a medical emergency."

They literally had every piece of equipment known to man on this plane. Unfortunately, most of it was in the hold. And none of it was to treat a myocardial infarction.

She cracked open their first-aid kit, monitoring his blood pressure and giving him some aspirin. She pasted a smile on her face. "Things will be fine, Callum. We'll get you picked up at the airport and taken to the nearest cardiac unit."

His hand gripped her wrist. "I'm sorry, Callie. I shouldn't be leaving you to deal with this. Not with Sawyer. You two are like oil and water. You won't mix. Not at all." His head was shaking.

Callie's stomach was churning. The thought of facing the legendary Sawyer herself was not filling her with confidence. But right now she would do or say anything that would relieve the pressure on Callum. Anything at all.

"Everything will be fine. You'll see. Don't worry about a thing, Callum. I can handle Sawyer."

Famous last words.

CHAPTER TWO

"Who are you and where is Callum Ferguson?" Not waiting for an answer, the man with the shaggy hair pushed past her and looked behind her. With his broad frame and pale green eyes, on another occasion she might have looked twice. But she didn't have time for this.

Great. The welcoming party. And he was obviously delighted to see her.

She struggled to set the box down on the reception desk. There was only one person this could be. And she intended to start the way she meant to continue. This was business.

"Here are the N95 masks. Make sure anyone that goes into the room with those kids wears one. And make sure it's fitted properly, otherwise it will be useless."

He hadn't moved. He was still standing directly in her path. "I asked you a question."

She almost hesitated but that would do her no good. She needed to establish who was in charge here. And it was her.

"Matt Sawyer? I'm Callie Turner and I'm leading the team." She turned towards the door as the rest of the team fanned in behind her, carrying their equipment.

It was like an invasion. And the irony of that wasn't lost on her.

She tilted her head. "I'd shake your hand but you're already an infection control hazard, so forgive me."

Did she look confident? She certainly hoped so, because her stomach was churning so much that any minute now she might just throw up all over his Converses.

She walked around behind the desk and started pulling things out of the boxes being deposited next to her. "Lewis, Cheryl, set up here and here." She pointed to some nearby desks.

"I'm only going to ask you one more time. Where is Callum Ferguson?"

He was practically growling at her now. And that hair of his was going to annoy her. Why didn't he get a decent haircut? Wouldn't long hair be an infection control hazard? Maybe she should suggest he find an elastic band and tie it back, though on second thoughts it wasn't quite long enough for that.

She drew herself up before him. This man was starting to annoy her. *Did he think she was hiding Callum Ferguson in her back pocket?* "I'm sorry to tell you, Dr. Sawyer, that Dr. Ferguson became unwell on the plane en route."

He actually twitched. As if she'd just said something to shock him. Maybe he was a human being after all.

"What happened?"

"We think he had an MI. He's been taken to the cardiac unit at St John's. I heard it's the best in town."

She waited for a second while he digested the news. Would he realize she'd checked up on the best place to send her colleague, rather than just send him off to the nearest hospital available? She hoped so. From the expression on Sawyer's face she might need to win some points with him.

Why did the thought of being quarantined with this man fill her with impending doom?

Sawyer was about to explode. And Miss Hoity-Toity with her navy-blue suit, pointy shoes and squinty hairdo was first in line to bear the brunt of the impact.

It was bad enough that he was here—but now to find out that the one person in the DPA he absolutely trusted *wasn't* going to be here?

The thought of Callum Ferguson having an MI was sickening. Sawyer had almost fallen into the trap of thinking the man was invincible. He'd spent the last forty years investigating outbreaks and coming home unscathed.

Please let him be okay.

He scowled at Callie Turner as she issued orders to those all around him. Did she realize her hand was trembling ever so slightly? Because he did. And it wasn't instilling him with confidence.

He planted his hand on his hip. "How old are you *exactly?*"

He could see her bristling. Her brain was whirring, obviously trying to think up a smart answer. She walked straight over to him and put both of her hands on her hips, mirroring his stance.

"Exactly how old do you want me to be, Sawyer?"

He couldn't wipe the smile from his face. Smart and sassy—if a little young. The girl showed promise.

"So what happened to the hair?"

He'd already caught her tugging self-consciously at one side of her hair. As if she wasn't quite used to it yet. "Were you halfway through when you took my call?"

He took a piece of gum offered by nearby Miriam and started chewing as he watched her. He could tell she was irritated by him. Perfect. Maybe if he annoyed Miss DPA enough, he could get out of here.

Except it didn't work like that and he knew it. Still, he could live in hope.

She dumped a final pile of papers on the desk from her box, which she picked up and kicked under the desk. Yip. She was definitely mad.

She grabbed the heavily clipped document on the top of the pile, strode over and thrust it directly against his chest. It hit him square in the solar plexus, causing him to catch his breath.

"My haircut cost more than you probably make in a month. Now, here—read this. And it isn't from me. It's from Callum. He said to make sure it was the first thing I gave you—along with the instructions to follow it to the letter."

He pulled the document off his chest. The DPA plan for a smallpox outbreak. All three hundred pages of it. He let it go and it skidded across the desk towards her.

"I don't need to read this."

She stepped back in front of him. "Yes. You do. You've already broken protocol once today, Dr. Sawyer. You should have contacted the state department *before* you contacted us. But, then, you know that, don't you? You don't work for the DPA anymore, Dr. Sawyer."

He cracked his chewing gum. "Well, that's at least one thing we agree on."

She glanced at her watch. "So, that means, that as of right now—five thirty-six p.m.—you work for me. You, and everyone else in here. This is my hospital now, Dr. Sawyer, my jurisdiction, and you will do exactly what I tell you." She jerked her thumb over her shoulder. "And it's all in that plan. So memorize it because there'll be a pop quiz later."

She kicked her navy-blue platforms beneath the desk and started to undo her shirt. "Where are the scrubs and protective clothing?" she shouted along the corridor.

"In here," came a reply from one of the nearby rooms.

"Let's go see these kids," she barked at Sawyer over her shoulder as she headed to the room.

Organized chaos was continuing around him. Piles upon piles of paper were being pulled from boxes, new phones were appearing and being plugged in all around him. He recognized a couple of the faces—a few of the epidemiologists and contact tracers—standing with their clipboards at the ready.

He could hear the voices of the admin staff around him. "No, put it here. Callie's very particular about paperwork. Put the algorithms up on the walls, in the treatments rooms and outside the patient rooms. Everyone has to follow them to the letter."

So, she was a rules-and-regulations girl? This was about to get interesting.

He wandered over to the room. Callie was standing in her bra and pants, opening a clean set of regulation pale pink scrubs. Last time he'd worn them they'd been green. Obviously a new addition to the DPA repertoire.

The sight made him catch his breath. It was amazing what could lurk beneath those stuffy blue suits and pointy shoes. The suit was lying in a crumpled heap on the ground, discarded as if it were worthless when it easily clocked in at over a thousand dollars. He could see the label from here. Maybe Miss Hoity-Toity did have some redeeming features after all.

Her skin was lightly tanned, with some white strap

marks on her shoulders barely covered by her bra. She was a matching-set girl. Pale lilac satin. But she didn't have her back to him so from this angle he couldn't tell if she favored briefs or a thong...

Her stomach wasn't washboard flat like some women he'd known. It was gently rounded, proving to him that she wasn't a woman who lived on salad alone. But the most intriguing thing about her was the pale white scar trailing down the outside of her leg. Where had that come from? It might be interesting to find out. His eyes lifted a little higher. And as for her breasts...

"Quit staring at me." She pulled on her scrub trousers. "You're a doctor. Apparently you've seen it all before." She tossed him a hat. "And get that mop of yours hidden."

She pulled her scrub top over her head and knelt in the corner next to her bag. She seemed completely unaffected by his gawping. Just as well really.

Sawyer reluctantly pulled on the hat and a disposable pale yellow isolation gown over his scrubs. She appeared at his side a few seconds later as he struggled to tuck his hair inside the slightly too big cap.

"Want one of these?" She waved a bobby pin under his nose with a twinkle in her eye. She was laughing at him.

"Won't you need all of them to pull back that one side of your bad haircut?"

She flung a regulation mask at him. "Ha. Ha. Now, let's go."

They walked down the corridor where the lights were still dimmed. She paused outside the door, her hand resting lightly on his arm.

"Let's clarify before we go in. How many staff have been in contact with these kids?"

He nodded. He would probably answer these questions a dozen times today. "Main contact has been myself and Alison, one of our nurses. We're estimating they were only in the waiting room around ten minutes. One of the triage nurses moved them through to a room quickly as the kids were pretty sick."

Her eyebrows rose above her mask. "I take it that you've continued to limit the contact to yourselves?"

"Ah, about that."

"What?" Her expression had changed in an instant. Her eyes had narrowed and her glare hardened.

"There's a problem."

"What kind of problem?"

"Alison's pregnant. Eighteen weeks."

She let out an expression that wasn't at all ladylike. He hadn't known she had it in her.

"Exactly. I haven't let her go back in. She's adamant. Says there's no point exposing anyone else to something she's already breathed in anyway. But I wasn't having any of it."

He could see her brain racing. There was the tiniest flicker of panic under that mask. "But the vaccine…"

He touched her shoulder. "I know. We don't know the effects it could have on a fetus." He shrugged. "I don't know if you've come up with any new research in the last six years, but I wouldn't want to be the doctor to give it to her."

She nodded. "Leave it with me. I'll take it up with the team." She turned back to the room. "We need to get some samples."

"It's already done."

"What?" She whipped around. "Why didn't you say so?"

He sighed. "What do you think I've been doing these

last few hours? I'm not that far out of the loop that I don't know how to take samples. Besides, the kids were used to me. It was better that I did it."

She nodded, albeit reluctantly. "And the parents?"

"I've taken samples from them too. They're all packaged and ready to go. Let's find out what we're dealing with."

"I want to see the kids first."

Now she was annoying him. "You think I made their spots up? Drew them on their faces and arms?"

"Of course I don't. But, like or not, I'm the doctor in charge here. I need to see the spots for myself. Get some better pictures than the ones snapped on your phone. I need to be clear that you've ruled out everything."

She was only saying what he would have said himself a few years ago. She was doing things by the book. But in his eyes, doing things by the book was wasting time. That was why he hadn't bothered with the call to the state department. Best to go right to the source.

And this family might not have that time to waste. Just like his hadn't.

It made him mad. Irrationally mad. And it didn't matter that the voices in his head were telling him that. Because he wasn't listening.

"For goodness' sake. Don't you have any confidence in my abilities? I've been doing this job since you were in kindergarten. I could run rings around you!"

She pushed her face up next to his. If it weren't for the masks, their noses would be practically touching. "You're not quite that old, Matt Sawyer. And it doesn't matter what I think about your doctoring abilities. I'm in charge here. Not you. We've already established you don't work for the DPA any more and I do. You know how things work. You know the procedures and protocols. You might not have followed them but I do. To the letter." She put her hand on the door. "Now, do your job, Dr. Sawyer. Take me in there and introduce me to the parents."

Callie leaned back against the wall in the sluice room. She'd just pulled off her disposable clothing and mask and dispensed with them in line with all the infection control protocols.

She let the temperature of the cool concrete seep through her thin scrub top. Thank goodness. With the air-conditioning turned off this place was getting warm. Too warm. Why couldn't this outbreak have happened in the middle of the winter, when Chicago was knee deep in snow, instead of when it was the height of summer? It could have made things a whole lot simpler for them. It could also have made the E.R. a whole lot quieter.

Those kids were sick. Sawyer hadn't been kidding. They were *really* sick. She'd really prefer it if they could be in a pediatric intensive care unit, but right now that was out of the question.

And even though it seemed like madness, in a few minutes' time she was going to have to inoculate them and their parents with the smallpox vaccine.

Then she was going to have to deal with the staff, herself included.

There wasn't time to waste. The laboratory samples were just away. It could be anything up to forty-eight hours before they had even a partial diagnosis and seven days before a definitive diagnosis. She didn't want to wait that long.

She knew that would cause problems with Sawyer. He would want to wait—to be sure before they inflicted a vaccine with known side-effects on people who might not be at risk. But she'd already had that conversation with her boss, Evan Hunter. He'd told her to make the decision on the best information available. And she had.

She wrinkled her nose, trying to picture the relationship between the man she'd just met and Callum Ferguson, a doctor for whom she had the utmost respect. How on earth had these two ever gotten along? It just didn't seem feasible.

She knew that Sawyer had lost his pregnant wife on a mission. That must have been devastating. But to walk away from his life and his career? Why would anyone do that? Had he been grief stricken? Had he been depressed?

And more to the point, how was he now? Was he reliable enough to trust his judgment on how best to proceed? Because right now what she really needed was partner in crime, not an outright enemy.

If only Callum were here. He knew how to handle Sawyer. She wouldn't have needed to have dealt with any of this.

Her fingers fell to her leg—to her scar. It had started to itch. Just as it always did when she was under stress. She took a deep breath.

She'd made a decision. Now it was time to face the fallout.

"Are you crazy?"

"No. I'm not crazy. I've already spoke to my boss at the DPA. Funnily enough, he didn't want you sitting in on that conference call. It seems your reputation has preceded you."

"I don't care about my reputation—"

"Obviously."

"I care about these staff."

He spun around as the crates were wheeled into the treatment room and the vaccine started to be unloaded. One of the contact tracers came up and mumbled in her ear, "We're going to start with a limited number of people affected. The kids, their parents, Dr. Sawyer, yourself and these other four members of staff who've had limited contact."

"What about Alison?"

The contact tracer hesitated, looking from one to the other. "That's not my decision," he said as he spun away.

Callie swallowed. She could do with something cool to drink, her throat was dry and scratchy. "Alison will have to make her own decision on the vaccine. There isn't enough data for us to give her reliable information."

She saw the look on his face. He looked haunted. As if he'd just seen a ghost from the past. Was this what had happened to his wife? Had she been exposed to something that couldn't be treated because of her pregnancy? This might all be too close to home for Matt Sawyer.

"Okay." He ran his fingers through his hair. It hadn't got any better now it had been released from the cap. In fact, it seemed to have grown even longer. "Do me a favor?"

She lifted her head from the clipboard she was scribbling on. "What?"

"Let me be the one to talk to Alison about it. If there hasn't been any more research in the last six years, then I'm as up to date as you are."

She took a deep breath. She didn't know this guy well enough to know how he would handle this. He was obviously worried about his colleague. But was that all? And would his past experience affect his professional judgment?

"You can't recommend it one way or the other, you understand that, don't you?"

She could tell he wanted to snap at her. To tell her where to go. But something made him bite his tongue. "I can be impartial. I'll give her all the facts and let her make her own decision. It will come better from someone she knows."

Callie nodded. He was right. The smallpox vaccine came with a whole host of issues. She was already questioning some of the decisions that she'd made.

Alison was at the end of the corridor in a room on her own, partly for her own protection and partly for the protection of others. She'd been in direct contact with the disease—without any mask to limit the spread of the infection. In theory, because she hadn't had prolonged exposure in a confined space, she should be at low risk. But she'd also been exposed to—and had touched—the erupting spots. The most infectious element of the disease. Pregnant or not, she had to be assessed as being at risk. "You know I have to do this, right?"

He was glaring at her, his head shaking almost imperceptibly—as if it was an involuntary act.

"We have the three major diagnostic criteria for smallpox. This is a high-risk category. Those parents look sick already. They're probably in the prodromal stage of the disease."

The implication in the air was there, hanging between them. If they waited, it could result in more casualties and the DPA being slaughtered by the media for wasting time. That was the last thing anyone wanted.

"Callie? We have a problem."

Both heads turned to the DPA contact tracer standing at the door. "What is it, Hugo?"

She stepped forward and took the clipboard from his hand.

"It's the parents. They can't say for sure if the rash came out during or after the plane trip home."

"You're joking, right?" Callie felt the hackles rise on the back of her neck. This was one of the most crucial pieces of information they needed. Once the rash was out, the person was infectious. This was the difference between three hundred passengers on a plane being at risk or not.

Hugo looked pale. "Mrs. Keating is sure they didn't have a rash before they got on the plane. And she's almost sure they didn't have it on the plane, because the kids slept most of the journey. They went straight home and put the kids to bed—she didn't even get them changed. It wasn't until the next day she noticed the rash, but it could have been there on the plane."

Callie cringed, as Sawyer read her mind. "Prodromal stage. Did they sleep because they were developing the disease or did they sleep because it was a long flight?" He put a hand on Hugo's shoulder. "You have to establish if she noticed either of the kids having a fever during the journey." He paused, then added, "And make sure they didn't change planes anywhere." Sawyer rolled his eyes to the ceiling, "Or our contact tracing will become a nightmare."

Hugo nodded and disappeared back through the door.

Sawyer watched her as she fiddled with the clips in her hair. She was consulting the plan again. There seemed to be one in every room he entered. A list of procedures. A multitude of flow charts.

She didn't like it when things weren't exactly to plan.

Then again, she'd never been in charge of an epidemic before.

He could be doing so much more for her. He could be talking her through all this, helping her out. Liaising more with the team back at the DPA—even if that did mean dealing with Evan Hunter.

He knew all this stuff inside out and back to front.

But he just couldn't.

It didn't matter that he was stuck in the middle of all this. There was a line he didn't want to cross. He had to take a step back. He had to focus on the sick children.

He picked up another disposable gown and mask. "The IV fluids on the kids probably need changing. I'm going to go and check on them." He paused and turned his head just as he left. "You need to go and make an announcement to all the staff. You need to bring them up to date on the information that you have." He hesitated, then added something else.

"It's not only the natives that will be getting restless. We've got patients here who've been quarantined. They won't understand what's going on. They won't know what to tell their relatives."

She gave the slightest nod, as if the thought of what she was going to say was pressing down on her shoulders. He almost withered. "There's a public address system at the front desk—use that."

His phone beeped and he headed out of the room and down the corridor, pulling the phone from his pocket.

Violet.

He should have known.

No, he should have texted her first. She must be frantic.

He flicked the switch to silent and pushed it back into his pocket. She would just have to wait. He would deal with her later.

* * *

Callie could hear the raised voices as she strode down the corridor. "Why can't I leave? I'm fine. If I stay here, I'll get sick. You can't make me stay!"

It was inevitable. People always reacted like this when there was an outbreak. It was human nature.

The hard part was that Callie didn't want to be here any more than they did. But she couldn't exactly say that, could she?

The reality check was starting to sink in. She was in a strange city, in the middle of a possible outbreak of a disease that had supposedly been eradicated. She wasn't ready for this. If she closed her eyes for just a second, she could see Isabel in the middle of all this. This had been her dream from childhood—to work at the DPA at the cutting edge of infectious disease. She wouldn't be feeling like this. She wouldn't be feeling sick to her stomach and wanting to go and hide in a corner. Isabel would be center stage, running everything with a precise touch.

But Isabel wasn't here.

And that was Callie's fault. Her beautiful older sister had died six years earlier. Callie had been behind the wheel of their old car, taking a corner too fast—straight into the path of someone on the wrong side of the road. If only she hadn't been distracted—been fighting with her sister. Over something and nothing.

That was the thing that twisted the most. It was the same argument they'd had for years. Pizza or burgers. Something ridiculous. Something meaningless. How pathetic.

She fixed her gaze on the scene ahead. Isabel would know exactly how to handle a man like Sawyer. She would have had him eating out of her hand in five minutes flat.

Okay, maybe not five minutes.

Sawyer probably wasn't the type.

But, then, Isabel had been a people person. She'd known how to respond to people, she'd known how to work a crowd. All the things that Callie didn't have a clue about.

The voices were rising. Things were reaching a crescendo.

It was time to step up. Whether she liked it or not, it was time to take charge.

She pushed her way through the crowd around the desk and jumped up onto the reception area desk. "Is this the PA system?"

The clerk gave her a nod as she picked up the microphone and held it to her mouth. Adrenaline was starting to course through her system. All eyes were on her. She could do this. She pressed the button on the microphone and it let out a squeal from automatic feedback. Anyone who hadn't been listening before was certainly listening now.

"Hi, everyone. I'm sure you know I'm Callie Turner from the DPA. Let me bring you up to speed."

The anxiety in the room was palpable. The eyes staring at her were full of fear.

"You all know that we're dealing with two suspected cases of smallpox. That's the reason why the E.R. has been closed and we've enforced a quarantine. The samples have been collected and sent to the DPA lab for identification. The laboratory tests for smallpox are complicated and time-consuming. We should hear back in around forty-eight hours what type of virus it is— whether it's a type of pox or not—but it takes longer to identify what strain of virus it is. That can take any-thing up to seven days. So, until we know if it's a pox or not, we need to stay here. We need to try and contain this virus."

"I don't want to be in isolation," one of the men shouted.

"You're not," Callie said quickly. "You're quarantined—there's a difference. Isolation means separating people who are ill with a contagious disease from healthy people. The children who are affected have been isolated. Quarantine restricts the movement of people who have been exposed to someone or something, to see if they will become ill. That's what we're doing with all of you." Her hand stretched out across the room.

She could still feel the tension. Anxious glances being exchanged between staff and patients. She could see the questions forming on their lips. Best to keep going.

She tried to keep her voice calm. "The incubation period for smallpox is around twelve days but it can range from seven to seventeen days. Smallpox is spread person to person by droplet transmission. It can also be spread by contact with pustules or rash lesions or contaminated clothing or bedding.

"A person with smallpox is considered infectious when the rash appears, but at the moment we're going to consider any affected person infectious from the onset of fever. This should help us control any outbreak. It's important to remember that only close contacts—those who were within six or seven feet of the infectious person should be at risk."

She was talking too quickly, trying to put out too much information at once. She was hoping and praying that someone wouldn't pick up on the fact that they could be quarantined together for seventeen days.

"Should? What do you mean, 'should'? Don't you know?"

Callie took a deep breath. She didn't blame people for being angry. She would be angry too. But as she opened her mouth to speak, Sawyer got in there first. He'd appeared out of nowhere, stepping up alongside her, his hand closing over hers as he took the PA microphone from her.

"This isn't like some disaster movie, folks. A person with smallpox doesn't walk, coughing and spluttering, through a crowd and infect everyone around them. For a start, most people infected with smallpox don't cough anyway. And the last data available from the DPA shows that the average person affected can infect around five to seven people. And those would only be the close contacts around them. Let's not panic. Let's keep this in perspective."

She was watching him, her breath caught her in throat. He was doing what *she* should be doing. He was keeping calm and giving them clear and easy-to-understand information.

Part of her felt angry. And part of her felt relief.

She was out of her depth and she knew it.

The DPA was a big place. And she was a good doctor—when she was part of a team. But as a leader? Not so much.

Put her in a room with a pile of paperwork and she was the best. Methodical, good at interpreting the practical applications of a plan.

She could do the patient stuff—she could, obviously, or she wouldn't have made it through medical school or her residency. Actually, some of it she had loved. But she'd enjoyed the one-to-one patient contacts, patients a physician could take time with, understand their condition and give them long-term advice. Not the hurried, rushed, wide perspective of the DPA.

But, then, the DPA had been Isabel's dream, not hers. She'd never wanted this for herself.

And now? She was stuck with it.

"So, that's it folks. We'll let you know as soon as we hear back from the labs. In the meantime, we'll have arrangements in place to make everyone more comfortable with the facilities we have here." He raised his eyebrows at her. "It could be that in a few hours we move to somewhere more suitable?"

She nodded wordlessly. He must have known that Callum would already have put the wheels in motion to set up a category C facility for containment.

"In the meantime, follow the infection control procedures on the walls around you. Take a deep breath and show a little patience. We're all scared." He pointed at the figures lining the walls with their clipboards, "It's important we help these guys out. Tell them everything you know." He looked back at Callie. She was sure that right now she must resemble a deer caught in a set of headlights. "And if you have any questions, Dr. Turner is in charge. That's it for now."

He jumped off the table and headed back down the corridor.

The room was quieter now, the shouting had stopped. Her legs were trembling and she grabbed hold of a hand offered to her as she climbed down off the table. Heads were down, people working away, going about their business. One of the security guards was helping one of the nursing aides carry linen through to another room to help set up some beds.

Callie knew she couldn't leave this. She knew she

had to talk to him. Even though he was trying to put some space between them.

"Sawyer." She was breathless, running down the corridor after him. "I just wanted to say thank you. For back there."

His green eyes fixed on hers, just for a second, before they flitted away and he ran his fingers through that hair again. Her heart clenched, even though she couldn't understand why. He was exasperated with her. "That was a one-off, Callie. Don't count on me to help you again." He turned and strode back down the corridor, leaving her standing there.

Alone.

CHAPTER THREE

"YOU NEED TO manage things better." He couldn't help it. There were probably a million other ways to put this more delicately, but Sawyer didn't have time to think about nicer words.

Her head shot upwards. There it was—that rabbit-in-the-headlights look again from her.

He hated it. Because it made his stomach churn. He didn't know whether to be irritated by it or whether he really wanted to go over and give her a quick hug.

"What on earth do you mean, *'manage things better'*?" She made quote marks in the air with her fingers as she repeated his words back to him. He could see the lines across her brow. She was tired and she was stressed. And he understood that. It was part and parcel of the job at the DPA.

He could feel his lips turn upwards. She looked even prettier when she was cross.

"What are you smirking at?" She stood up from behind the desk. A desk lost under a multitude of piles of papers—no doubt more copies of plans and protocols. A few sheets scattered as she stood.

His smile broadened. He could tell she really wanted to stop and pick them up.

She was in front of him now, her hands on her hips. "What?"

He liked that. Sometimes she just got straight to the point. No skirting around the edge of things.

He gestured to the door behind him. "You need to clarify some things about the vaccination. There are still a lot of questions out there."

She sighed and ran her fingers through the short side of her hair. "I know. I'll get to it. I've got a million and one things to deal with." Her eyes flickered in the direction of the hidden desk.

"Then delegate."

She started, as if the thought of actually delegating horrified her.

"But I'm responsible—"

"And you need to be visible. You need to be seen. You have to be on the floor—not stuck in some office. You can make your decisions out there, not from behind a desk."

He could see her brain ticking, thinking over his suggestions. Truth be told, she'd been delegating from the minute she'd walked in the door—just not the important stuff.

"And you need to do something about Alison."

Her eyes narrowed. "I thought you wanted to deal with Alison."

"And I have—we've had the discussion about the vaccine. She hasn't decided what to do yet, but I think she'll opt on the side of caution and say no."

"So what's the problem?" She'd started to walk back over to the desk.

"The problem is she's a nurse. She's stuck in a room at the bottom of the corridor. Isolated. Quarantined—"

"You know that's not the case."

He touched her shoulder. "But she doesn't. You need to tell people, explain to them what the difference is. You explained that to the masses—but you need didn't explain it to her. She's in there frightened and alone. You need to communicate better." He could feel her bristle under his touch. "Alison needs to do something. I understand you think she might have been exposed but you can't leave her sitting there for hours on end." He picked up a pile of papers from the desk. "Give her a list of phone calls to make for you. Let her do some of the specialized phone contact tracing."

"She can't do that. That's a special skill. You need of hours of training to do that properly," she snapped.

He could feel the frustration rising in his chest. "It's only a list of questions! She's an intelligent human being. Give her something to do. Something to take her mind off things."

He grabbed the first random thought that entered his head. "Let her organize the food, then! Something—anything—to stop her thinking that if she hadn't come to work this morning she wouldn't have risked the life of her baby."

He could see the realization fall on her face. And suddenly he understood.

She was a big-picture girl. The perfect person for public health. She didn't individualize, or personalize, the other side of the job. The things that affected normal people.

He took a deep breath. He wasn't trying to make this harder for her. He knew she'd been thrown in at the deep end.

Part of him wanted to offer to take over, even though he knew that would never be allowed to. And part of him still wanted to run for the hills.

He hated this. Everything about this situation grated on him. He'd thought he'd be safe.

He'd thought he'd distanced himself enough to never to be in a situation like this again. How often did an E.R. notify an outbreak on this scale? Rarely.

And this type of disease? Well, let's face it, not in the last thirty or forty years.

No matter what his brain told him, he would not allow himself to be dragged in. Even though he was right in the middle of everything he needed to keep some distance. He needed *not* to have responsibility for this outbreak.

She was hesitating. He could see it written all over her face. Then the decision was made. It was almost as if he could see a little light go on behind her eyes.

She looked him square in the eye. "You're right. I can give her something to do. Something that means she's not at risk to herself or anyone else around her." She picked up a list from her desk. "She can order the food supplies, linen supplies and any extra medical supplies that we might need. The food's turned into a bit of a nightmare in the last few hours." She picked up a hefty manual from her desk, ripped out a few sheets and attached them to a red clipboard. "This will tell her everything she needs to know about how to arrange the delivery of supplies that keeps all parties safe."

Her eyes swept around the room.

It was almost as if once she'd made a decision, that was it. She was ready. She was organized. The courage of her convictions took her forward. She could be great at this job, if only she had confidence in her abilities. And she would get that. It would just take a few years.

A few years that she would normally have had in the DPA, working with their most experienced doctors.

His thoughts went back to Callum and he glanced at his watch. "I need to make a phone call."

Her hand rested on his arm. The warmth of her fingers stopped him dead.

"I need you to do one more thing for me before you go."

She was looking at him with those big eyes. The ones he preferred not to have contact with. This was where his gut twisted and he wanted to say no. Say no to anything that would drag him further into this mess.

There was a new edge to her voice, a new determination. She handed him a file from the desk. "I need you to look over this with an independent eye. You've been out of the DPA long enough to make an assessment."

He was confused now. What was she talking about? Instinctively, his hand reached out for the file.

"You told me to delegate. Everyone thought the next smallpox outbreak would be deliberate—a terrorist act. Nothing we've seen here supports that. All the information from the parents and contacts would lead me to suggest this was a natural outbreak—however impossible or improbable that may be."

He was nodding slowly. It was one of the first things that Callum had asked him. It was one of the most immediate priorities for the DPA: to try and determine the source.

"I need you to look over the rest of the evidence the contact tracers have collected. I have to phone Evan Hunter in the next half-hour. It's my professional opinion that this isn't a terrorist act." Her voice was wavering slightly. This was one of the most crucial decisions she would make in her lead role for the DPA.

Everything she was saying made sense and he knew that she would have read and analyzed the evidence to the best of her abilities. But time was pressing. If there was any threat to the general population, they had to know now.

He understood what this meant to her. And he understood why she was asking him.

It wasn't just that he'd told her to delegate. It was that this could impact on everything. The actions and reactions the world would have to this outbreak.

She had to be right.

She had to be sure.

If Callum had been here, this would have been on his head. But even then, he would have had Callie to bat things back and forth with. To agree with his decision-making.

She didn't have that.

She didn't have anyone.

So she was asking the one person here who might have those skills.

He laid his hand over hers. "I'll make the phone call. It will take two minutes and then I'll close this office door and look over all this information. If I have even a shadow of a doubt, I'll let you know."

Her shoulders sagged just a little. As if she'd just managed to disperse a little of their weight. "Thank you," she said as she walked out the door.

Sawyer watched her leave, trying not to look at her rear view in the pink scrubs. He couldn't work out what was going on. One minute she was driving him crazy. The next?

He slumped back in the chair a little, the mound of paper in front of him looking less than enticing. His phone slipped from his pocket and clattered to the floor.

It was like an alarm clock going off in his head.

Violet. He really needed to contact Violet.

His sister worked at the DPA and must be going crazy. She would have heard his name bandied about by now and know that he must be in the middle of all this.

His phone had been switched to silent for the last few hours and he glanced at the screen and cringed. He'd known as soon as he'd called the DPA that his number would have been logged in their system.

It made sense that she'd tried to get in touch with him—after all, he'd changed his number numerous times in the last few years—only getting in touch when he could face it.

He really didn't want to know how many missed calls and text messages he'd had from her. It just made him feel even guiltier.

When his wife had died and he'd walked away from the DPA, he'd also more or less walked away from his family.

It had been the only way he could cope.

He couldn't bear to have any reminders of Helen, his wife. It had been just too much. He'd needed time. He'd needed space.

On occasion—when he'd felt guilty enough—he'd send Violet a text just to let her know that he was safe. Nothing more. Nothing less.

She deserved better and he knew that. He just hadn't been in a position to give it.

The one saving grace was that no one in the DPA knew they were related. She'd started just after he'd left. And the last thing any new doctor needed was to live in the shadow of the family black sheep.

He turned the phone over in his hands and looked at his watch. The mountain of paper on the desk seemed to have mysteriously multiplied in the last few minutes.

He would phone Violet. He would.

But right now time was critical. He had to do this first.

Callie was mad.

But she was trying not to show it.

Everything he'd said was right.

The doctor who was apparently bad-tempered and temperamental was making her feel as if she was the problem and not him.

The worst thing was he'd sounded clear-headed and rational. He was right, she did need to delegate. No matter how alien the concept seemed to her.

So she'd delegated the most obvious duty to him. Evan Hunter would have a fit.

But she was in charge here. Not him. And since Callum wasn't here, she had to rely on the one member of staff who had some experience in this area—whether Evan Hunter liked it or not.

"Callie?"

She'd reached the treatment room. One of the second-year residents was emptying the refrigerated container of vaccines.

"What is it?"

"How many of these do you want me to draw up?"

She shook her head. "None—yet." She glanced at the face of the resident, who was obviously worried about doing anything wrong. A few years ago that would have been her.

"Have you used the ring vaccination concept before?"

The resident shook her head.

In the midst of all this madness Callie had to remember she had a responsibility to teach. To help the staff around her learn their roles. To lead by example.

The words started repeating to a rhythm in her head.

"Ring vaccination controls an outbreak by vaccinating and monitoring a ring of people around each infected individual. The idea is to form a buffer of immune individuals to prevent the spread of the disease. It's a way of containment."

"And it works effectively?"

Callie gave a small smile. "We thought it did. Ring vaccination was held as essential in the eradication of smallpox. For the vast majority of people, getting the smallpox vaccine within three days of exposure will significantly lesson the severity of the symptoms."

"What about people who were vaccinated before against smallpox? Aren't they already protected?"

Callie shook her head. "It's a common misconception. Why do you ask?"

"One of the men in the waiting room said he'd had the vaccination as a child and he wouldn't need anything."

Callie smiled. "Last time ring vaccination was used for smallpox was in the late seventies. But if he was vaccinated then, he would only have had protection for between three and five years. There might still be some antibodies in his blood but we can't assume anything."

"Would we vaccinate him again?"

"It depends where he falls at risk. In the first instance, we vaccinate anyone who has been, or may have been, exposed to someone who has the infection."

"He was sitting next to the family in the waiting room."

Callie nodded. There was so much about this that wasn't written entirely in stone and open to interpretation. "Then we need to assess how much contact he had with the family—and for how long."

"And that's where all the guessing games start."

The deep voice at the door made her head jerk up. Sawyer was standing with her file in his hand. He walked over and held it out towards her. "You're right, Callie. It didn't take long to review the information." He shook his head. "There's absolutely nothing there to hint at anything other than a natural outbreak—the very thing the DPA declared could never happen."

The sense of relief that rushed over her body was instant. She'd been scared. Scared that she'd missed something—that she'd overlooked something important. Something her sister would never have done.

It was the first time today she actually felt as if she might be doing a good job.

She took the file from his hand. "I guess we don't know everything, then," she murmured.

He gave her a lazy smile and raised one eyebrow at her. "Really? You mean the DPA hasn't managed to find its way into every corner of the universe to see if there are any deadly diseases left?"

Her eyes were scanning the sheets in front of her. She shrugged. "It makes sense. The Keatings said that it was the first time the locals had come into contact with outsiders."

"First contact. Sounds much sexier than it should."

She raised her eyebrows at him. "Sounds like a whole can of worms."

The resident lowered her head and busied herself in the corner of the room. In some ways Callie wanted to do that too.

She wanted to take herself out of the range of Sawyer's impenetrable stare. It was making her hair stand on end and sending weird tingles down her spine.

She felt like a high-school teenager on prom night, not an experienced doctor in the midst of an emergency situation.

She picked up one of the vials on the countertop. "I guess I should lead by example."

He was at her side in an instant. "What do you mean?"

"If I'm going to recommend first-line vaccination, I guess I should go first."

"Are you sure about this?"

Callie almost laughed out loud. Was he joking? "Of course I'm not sure. But I've got to base this on the evidence that I've got, no matter how imperfect it is. If this is smallpox, I've a duty of care to protect others and contain the virus. You, me, the parents—anyone else assessed as 'at risk' should be vaccinated."

She picked up the diluent and delivered it swiftly into the container holding the dried vaccine. Her hands rolled the vial between her palms, watching the liquid oscillate back and forth.

"I think you should wait. I think we should have a definite diagnosis before we start vaccinating."

She nodded. In an ideal world that made sense. But this wasn't an ideal world. It was a completely imperfect situation. If she hesitated, she put people at risk.

This was her decision. The buck stopped with her.

"There are risks attached to any vaccine but this vaccine was widely used and we've got a lot of data on the issues raised. I've reviewed our medical notes. There's nothing in my history, your history or the parents' that would prevent vaccination. The only issue is Alison— and she's already told me she's decided against it."

There was an expression on his face she couldn't

fathom. Something flickering behind his eyes, as if the thoughts in his head were about to combust.

This man was almost unreadable.

Was he relieved or mad? Did he want Alison to have the vaccine and put her baby at risk? Or did he want her to take her chances without?

Obviously, she knew the outcome—but that didn't help here.

Had Sawyer's wife been in similar circumstances and avoided a vaccine because she had been pregnant? Or had she taken a vaccine—that was untried and untested on pregnant women—with devastating consequences?

It was almost as if he'd gone on autopilot. He washed his hands, lifted a syringe and needle and tipped up the vial, plunging the needle inside and extracting the vaccine. "If this is what you want, let's do it."

She was stunned. She'd thought he was going to refuse—going to argue with her some more and storm off. This was the last thing she'd expected.

"Are you going to get vaccinated?"

He nodded almost imperceptibly. "Of course."

She tilted her head and raised her eyebrows at him, the question obvious.

"I'm working on the assumption you're going to say that only vaccinated personnel can work with the kids. These kids are mine. They're *my* patients. I won't let you keep me out. And if a vaccine is what it takes…" he shrugged "…so be it."

The words were stuck in her throat now.

The thing that seemed to pass her by. The people thing.

The thing she really wanted to concentrate on, but her

public health role wouldn't let her. She'd learned over the years just to lock it away in a corner of her mind.

But it was the thing that was on the forefront of *his* mind. And it was affecting his reactions. If only she could have the same freedom.

He was prepared to take a vaccine with known side-effects in order to keep looking after these children.

And no matter how hard she tried not to, she had to admire him for it.

There was only one thing she could do.

She turned her arm towards him. "Let's do it." Her voice sounded confident, the way she wanted to appear to the outside world. Her insides were currently mush.

His finger ran down the outside of her upper arm. Totally unexpected. The lightest of touches. She heard his intake of breath before he went back to standard technique and pinched her skin.

It was over in the blink of an eye. She never even felt the bifurcated needle penetrate her skin. It wasn't like a traditional shot and she felt the needle prick her skin a number of times in a few seconds before it was quickly removed and disposed of.

"You know this won't be pretty, don't you?"

She nodded, automatically reaching up and rubbing her arm. "I know what to expect. A red and itchy bump in a few days…" she rolled her eyes "…a delightful pus-filled blister in another week and then a scab."

She washed her hands at the sink as he drew up another dose of vaccine and handed it to her, pulling his scrub sleeve up above his shoulder. She could feel herself hesitate, taking in his defined deltoid and biceps muscles. Did Sawyer work out? He didn't seem the type.

"Something wrong?"

"What? No." She could feel the color flooding into

her cheeks. How embarrassing. He hadn't given her arm a second glance.

Concentrate. Focus. He was smirking at her again, almost as if he could see exactly what she was thinking.

She scowled, pinched his arm and injected him, delivering the vaccine in an instant. It was as quick as she could get this over and done with, so she could turn her back to dispose of the syringe.

"Ouch." He was rubbing his arm in mock horror. "It's all in the technique, you know."

"Yeah, yeah." She started washing her hands again. "You're not supposed to rub your arm, you know."

He shrugged. "Everyone does. It's an automatic response. Being a doctor doesn't make me any different." His arm was still exposed, and this time, instead of focusing on the muscle, her eyes focused on the skin.

It was full of little pock marks and lumps and bumps. The obvious flat scar from a BCG vaccination. He followed her eyes and gave her a grin. "A lifetime's work. Chicken pox as a child, then a whole career's worth of DPA vaccinations."

She pulled up her other sleeve. "Snap."

His finger touched her skin again and she felt herself suck in her breath as it ran over her BCG scar. He was standing just a little too close for comfort but seemed completely unaffected.

He turned and smiled at her. "At least you don't have chicken pox scars." Maybe it was the lazy way he said it or the way his smile seemed kind of sexy.

"Oh, I do. Just can't show them in public." She couldn't help it. The words were out before she had time to think about them. She was flirting. She was *flirting* with him. What was wrong with her?

That was the kind of response that her sister might

have given. The kind of response that had men eating out of the palm of her hand and following Isabel's butt with their eyes as she walked down the hallway.

But this was so *not* a Callie response.

What was she thinking of?

It wasn't that she was some shy, retiring virgin. She'd been on plenty of dates and had a number of relationships over the years. But she wasn't the type of girl who walked into a bar and flirted with a man. She was the kind of girl who met a man in a class or in a library, and went for a few quiet drinks before there was any touching, any kissing.

She wasn't used to being unnerved by a man. To find herself flustered and blushing around him. It made her cringe.

But Sawyer seemed immune. Maybe women flirted with him all the time? He just gave her a little wink and crossed the room. Now he was in midconversation with the second-year resident, explaining where some of the supplies were kept and how to access them.

He obviously didn't feel heat rising up the back of his neck to make him feel uncomfortable.

She took a deep breath and moved. Out to the madness of the corridor, where the incessant sound of phones ringing must be driving everyone mad.

She picked up the nearest one as she passed. The voice made her stop in her tracks.

"Callie? Is that you?"

Evan Hunter. It must be killing him to be stuck at Headquarters instead of being in the thick of things.

"Well?" His abrupt tone was hardly welcoming.

It was beginning to annoy her. Every phone call she'd had from this man had started with him snapping at her and shouting orders. Wasn't he supposed to be supporting her?

He knew she'd been flung in at the deep end.

"Hold on." She set down the phone, ignoring the expletives she could hear him yelling as she walked over to the whiteboard on the wall. The DPA team was well trained. Every piece of relevant information and the most up-to-date data was right in front of her. She didn't need to run around the department asking a barrage of questions.

She watched as a member of staff rubbed one number off the board and replaced it with another. The potential 'at risk' group was now at five. Not bad at all.

A list of queries had appeared around the containment facility. She would need to get onto them straight away.

The only glaring piece of information that was missing was around the plane. There was the number of passengers, with the number of contact details obtained. Three hundred passengers—with contact details for only seventy-six.

This was taking up too much of her team's time. They needed to deal with the issues around the containment facility. It was time to delegate.

She could feel her arm tremble slightly as she picked up the phone again. Isabel would have been fit for Evan Hunter. She would have chewed him up and spat him out. It was time to embrace some of her sister's personality traits.

"Evan?"

"What on earth were you doing? When I call I expect—"

She cut him off straight away. "What have I been doing? What have *I* been doing? I've just been getting my smallpox vaccination and I've just inoculated another member of staff. I've been assessing our most up-to-date information to determine whether or not this is a terrorist attack." She glanced at the clock. "Information I wasn't due to present to you for another eight minutes. And, incidentally, my professional opinion is that it's not.

"I've also been trying to keep the staff and patients here calm and informed about what's going on. I'm trying to find out how Callum is but no one will tell me anything. I'm having problems with the containment facility. We can't make all the contacts for the plane passengers." She was starting to count things off on her fingers.

"We're just about to vaccinate those exposed—but we have a pregnant nurse to consider. Oh, and Sawyer is driving me crazy." She took a deep breath. "So, how's your day going, Evan?" She couldn't help it. The more she spoke, the more she felt swamped, the more she felt angry that Callum wasn't at her side. The more she realized that Evan Hunter, boss or not, should be doing more to help her, not adding to the problems.

The silence at the end of the phone was deafening. Her heart rate quickened. Had she just got herself sacked?

No. How could he? Not when she was in the middle of all this.

She heard him clear his throat. "Point made."

She was shocked. "What?"

"Point made, Callie. What do you need?"

For a second she couldn't speak. *What did she need?* Apart from getting out of here?

"I need you to take over the plane contacts. We've got three hundred passengers and only contact details for seventy-six. I also need you to take over the viable threat assessment for these people as our details are sketchy. I'll get one of the contact tracers and epidemiologists to conference-call you." Isabel used to quote the English expression *"In for a penny, in for a pound"* before she took a risk. Somehow, it seemed apt.

"Fine. I can do that. Anything else?"

She felt like a girl in a fancy department store on a fifty percent sale day. But nothing else screamed out at her. "Can you magic me up some pediatric ICU facilities?"

"That might be a little tricky."

"Didn't think so. Never mind. I'll let you know if I need anything else. When can I expect to hear from the lab?"

"That's what I wanted to tell you."

Oops. She almost felt bad for being snarky with him.

"The samples have been received and are being processed. It's only been a couple of hours. In another ten we should be able to tell you which virus type it is. That will give us something to work with."

She nodded as she scribbled notes. "That's great."

"And, Callie?"

"Yes?" This was it. This was where he blasted her for the way she'd just spoken to him.

"Leave Sawyer to me. I'm going to try and find out where he's been and what he's been doing these last few years. Let him know who's in charge. Only use him if you have to. He's not part of the DPA anymore."

She could feel the steel in his words and instantly regretted her outburst that Sawyer was driving her crazy. "He's actually been quite helpful. He's just a little…" she struggled to think of the word "…inconsistent. One minute he's helping, the next he looks as if he could jump out the nearest window." She looked over at the window next to her. The sun was splitting the sky outside. She almost felt like jumping out the window herself and heading for the nearest beach. Chicago had good beaches, didn't it?

Her stomach rumbled loudly. What she wouldn't give for pizza right now.

Evan was still talking.

"Sorry, what?"

"I asked if you wanted another doctor sent in."

"No. Not right now. If things progress, then probably yes. But let's wait until we have the lab results. You're dealing with plane passengers and hopefully things are contained at our end."

Her brain started to whirr. She couldn't really understand why, in the midst of all this, part of his focus was on Sawyer. Surely Evan should just be grateful that she had any help at all? No matter how reluctant.

She rang off and stared at the phone. Her stomach rumbled again loudly. She didn't have time to figure that out right now.

Along with many other things, it would have to wait.

CHAPTER FOUR

"SAWYER? ARE YOU in here?" Callie stuck her head around the door into the darkened room. It was three a.m. and she could make out a heap bundled against the far wall, lying on a gurney.

The heap moved and groaned at her. "What?" He sat up and rubbed his eyes.

"Oh, I'm sorry," she whispered, searching the room for any other sleeping bodies. "Have you just got your head down?"

He swung his legs off the gurney and stood up, swaying a little. She walked across the room and put her arm on his. "I'm sorry, Sawyer. I didn't realize you were sleeping."

"I wasn't," he snapped.

She smiled at him. "Yes, you obviously were."

"What's wrong? Did something happen to the kids?" It was almost as if his brain had just engaged.

She tightened her grip on his arm. "No. I'm sorry. Nothing's changed. The kids are still pretty sick. Laura, one of the DPA nurses, is in with them now. I've kept Alison away, just like you said. She's still down at the other end of the corridor in a room on her own." She held up a paper bag and waved it under his nose. "She's doing a great job, by the way. She got me banana and toffee muffins."

"Oh, okay." The words took a few seconds to sink in then he scowled at her. "What is it, then?"

"It's Max Simpson, the chief of staff. It's three a.m. and I've just realized I haven't seen him yet. I've been so busy with things down here."

She could see the realization appear in his eyes. He grimaced.

"What is it?"

"Yeah. I meant to speak to you about Max too. I sort of made an executive decision there."

"You did what?" She was on edge again. What had he done now? He'd already broken protocol once. Had he done it again?

He shook his head. "I'm sorry, Callie, I meant to talk to you earlier. Max is the reason I'm here."

"What are you talking about? I don't understand."

"Max has prostate cancer. He's undergoing chemo-therapy—midway through a course. He's immuno-compromised. So I told him he can't be anywhere the possible threat of infection and he can't be near anyone we immunize—including us."

The words struck home. For a second she'd thought he was going to say something unreasonable—something to get her back up. Instead, Callie felt the tense-ness ease out of her muscles. Another piece of the jigsaw.

"So, what? You're covering for him right now?"

She could see the hesitation on his face. "Yes, I guess I am. Max was a real hands-on sort of guy. He dropped out of his clinical commitments a couple of months ago and has just been doing a few days' office work a week. He wants to keep his hand in during his treatment but couldn't manage any more. I was only supposed to be here for two weeks, covering someone's vacation leave. But I met Max, he liked me and asked me to stay and cover his clinical work in the E.R. for a few months."

She was trying to read behind the lines. Trying to understand the things that he wasn't telling her. She couldn't work this guy out at all.

Matt Sawyer's reputation had preceded him. Apparently when his wife had died, he'd had the mother of all temper tantrums, telling everyone around him what he really thought of them. She could only imagine that Evan Hunter had been one of them.

But here he was describing how he was helping out a sick colleague. Someone he'd only met a few months ago.

Was it just everyone at the DPA he hated? Did he blame them for his wife's death?

She could see him searching her face. Was he worried that she would be unhappy for him not putting her in the picture before now? Or was he worried she would actually see his human side? The side he'd tried to hide from her when he'd said his help had been a one-off event.

She wrinkled her nose at him. It was late and she was getting tired. Her defenses were weakening as she approached that hideous hour in the middle of the night when her body was screaming for her bed.

"I don't get you, Matt Sawyer," she whispered.

"What don't you get?" He took a step closer. The lights in the room were still out and the only light was from the corridor outside, sending a warm, comfortable glow over them both. He'd changed into the regulation DPA pale pink scrubs. Pink on a man. Whose idea had that been? He made them look good, though. Kind of inviting.

He reached up and gave one of her wayward locks at little tug, a sexy smile crossing his face, "This hair of yours, it's driving me crazy. I keep wanting to grab a pair of scissors and lop this off."

Her hand reached up too, brushing the side of his face and touching his brown hair that was mussed up around his ears. "Likewise," she whispered.

For a few seconds neither of them spoke. Callie had no idea what she was doing. She was in the middle of the biggest potential outbreak of her career, in a strange city, with no real idea of what could happen next. There was nothing in the plan about this. There was nothing that told you what to do when your colleague was sick and you had to take over the management of a situation like this. She needed a friend. She needed someone to reach out to.

"I saw your hand shaking earlier. Are you scared, Dr. Turner?" His voice was low, barely above a whisper. No one else could possibly hear them.

"Scared?" she repeated. "Matt, I'm terrified." She felt a whoosh of air come out of her lungs. It was the first time she'd said the words out loud. She'd spent the last twelve hours thinking them but she couldn't have imagined actually saying them to someone. It was like laying herself bare. To a man she hardly knew. It had to be a recipe for disaster.

He raised one eyebrow. "Like I said earlier, we're all scared. There's not a person in this E.R. right now who wants to be here—except, of course, for a few DPA geeks. Most people would sell their right arm to get out of here." He touched the side of her arm, running the palm of his hand up and down it. "Fear of the unknown is one of the most terrifying fears that there is."

She nodded, knowing what he was saying was true. There was something soothing about his voice. Something reassuring.

Her hand touched the side of his cheek. He almost flinched. She could see it. But he stood firm, his pale green eyes fixed on hers. "I can't work you out, Matt Sawyer. You're supposed to be a bad boy—a rule-breaker. Mr. Nasty. But right now I'm seeing a whole other side to you."

He wrinkled his nose. "What's that smell?"

"What smell?" She sniffed the air around her. "I can't smell anything."

"It's weird. Like strawberries or fruit or something."

She smiled. It was proof that they were standing too close to one another. "It's raspberries. It's my shampoo."

He moved even closer, his nose brushing against the top of her head as he inhaled again. "Almost good enough to eat," he murmured.

She couldn't wrap her head around all this. Maybe it was the time of night and her befuddled brain. She'd heard that Sawyer had lost it after his wife had died, had finished treating the patients he'd had to, had roared at everyone and walked off the job. He'd refused to make contact with anyone after that.

But here he was. Obviously struggling. But here.

His hand reached up and tightened around hers. There was an edge to his gaze. A shield going up right before her eyes. "What do you want to know?"

"I don't *know* that I want to know anything. I guess I just want to find out for myself. If I'd listened to Evan Hunter, I wouldn't have spoken to you at all when I got here, but I like to go on instincts."

"And what are your instincts telling you, Callie Turner?"

Wow. What a question. Because right now her instincts were telling her she was acting like a seventeen-year-old girl rather than a twenty-nine-year-old woman.

He moved their hands from the side of his cheek to resting both of them on her breastbone. Could he feel her heart beating against the skin on his hand? A man who had seen her virtually naked a few hours before?

What was she thinking about? Outside, down at the desk, there were a million things that she should be doing. Being in here, with Matt Sawyer, wasn't on the list that she'd prepared earlier.

But the words came too easily, "My instincts are telling me that Callum Ferguson is one of the wisest men I've ever known. And if he had hope for you, then maybe I should too."

He was even closer now. She could feel his breath on her cheeks, warming her skin. He bent forward, his lips brushing the side of her ear. It felt like the most erotic touch she'd ever experienced. "What if I told you I'm still a bad boy? What if I told you I left my last two jobs in Alaska and Connecticut before they could fire me?"

And then it happened. Callie just let go. Just like she'd done on the phone earlier with Evan. She didn't think, she just acted. She spoke the words that came instantly into her brain. *What was happening to her?* "I'd say you found problems in the places you were working. I'd say you told them what was wrong and how to fix it. I'd say they probably didn't like it."

He tilted his head to one side, the lazy smile still fixed on his face. "I knew you were young. I thought you didn't know anything. I thought you only followed rules."

His words were supposed to be teasing but something else happened.

Something flooded through her veins. Adrenaline, laced with fear.

She shouldn't be doing this. She shouldn't be in here with him. It was compromising her ability to think straight.

He was right. Following rules was what she knew. Following rules was *safe*.

Last time she hadn't followed the rules it had ruined her life.

No. It had ruined her *sister's* life.

So, getting involved with a rule-breaker?

Not an option.

His phone buzzed, in that gentle, quiet way it did when it was switched to vibrate instead of ring. She sprang backwards. "I need to go, Matt." She pushed the door open, flooding the room with light.

"Wait!" He grabbed her arm as he glanced at his phone. "I'm guessing here as I'm not sure of the number but I think it's my sister. She's the only person I know who would be so persistent."

"Your sister?" The words cut through her like a knife. Her back-to-reality jolt was instant. "You have a sister?"

Something had just happened. And Sawyer didn't understand it. One minute they'd been almost nose to nose in the darkened room—as if something was about to happen. The next minute he had almost seen her building the wall around herself.

He had no idea what had made her just snap like that.

Miss Hoity-Toity had looked almost inviting a minute ago. For a second he'd almost thought about…

No. Not possible. He didn't think like that any more.

Well, not unless he was in a bar and halfway through a bottle.

But for a few seconds she'd looked vulnerable. She'd looked like someone who could do with a hug. And he wasn't the hugging type.

And that smell from her. The raspberry shampoo. More enticing than any perfume he'd ever smelt.

It was weird what confined spaces could do to a person.

She was still looking at him with those too-wide eyes. What was with her? What was the big deal?

"Yes, I've got a sister."

"I meant to ask you if there was anybody you wanted to notify that you had been quarantined. Haven't you told her what's happened?"

His eyes fixed on the floor. This wasn't going to be pretty. "My sister's called Violet. Violet Connelly." He waited for the penny to drop.

And it did.

"Violet Connelly's your sister?" Her voice rose, filling the quiet room.

He leaned against the doorjamb and folded his arms. He was well aware he was trying to look laid back, but he was feeling anything but. All of a sudden he was hit by a wave of emotions that he didn't want to deal with. He tried to focus on the face in front of him. "Yes. Why so surprised?"

"Violet Connelly is your sister?"

"You've already said that and I've already answered."

She wrinkled her nose. It made her look kind of cute. "Why hasn't she said anything? I've never heard her mention you and I've been at the DPA for the last three years."

"I'm the family black sheep." Explanations weren't really his thing. It seemed the easiest solution.

"Bull. Violet's not like that at all."

Okay. Maybe not.

"And why don't you have your sister's number in your phone?"

He shifted uncomfortably. "I've been out of touch for a little while."

"With your sister?" Her voice rose in pitch. "How can you be out of touch with your sister?" Little pink spots had appeared on her cheeks.

"She has a different name. How come?"

"So now you're getting personal?"

"Don't get smart, Sawyer. You've just told me a woman I've worked alongside for the last three years is your sister. Violet's a sweetheart and she's never mentioned you once. Why?"

He shrugged. He really didn't want to have this conversation. It was way too uncomfortable. And it was bringing up a whole load of guilt that he really didn't want to consider. "It's complicated."

Now she looked angry. That middle-of-the-night woman angry. Never a good sign. "Don't give me the *'it's complicated'* crap." She raised her fingers in the air again. "Tell me why on earth she would keep something like that secret? Maybe Evan Hunter was right—maybe we should be looking a little closer at you."

He could feel the pent-up anger build in his chest. His temper was about to flare. Here. In the middle of the hospital. In the middle of a crisis situation.

He turned and flipped on the light, walking over to the nearby sink and running the cold tap. He bent over and started splashing water on his face. How dared she?

That was almost an implication that he was involved in this crisis situation.

This woman didn't know him at all. Didn't know anything but hearsay and gossip. If she knew even the tiniest part of him she'd know he'd do anything to get out of here.

He could feel the pressure building in his chest. Wasn't it bad enough that she'd just reminded him how guilty he felt about pushing his family—and his sister—away? He felt as if a truckload of concrete had just been dumped on his head.

As if this situation wasn't already bad enough.

Now she was making him think about things he'd spent the last six years pushing away.

He grabbed some paper towels and dried his face. Breathed in through his nose and out through his mouth. The flare was reducing. He didn't feel the urge to hit a wall any more. He was trying to think reasonable, rational thoughts.

But Callie Turner was still there. Wondering what she'd just witnessed.

He turned to face her. "Try walking in Violet's shoes for a while, Callie. Her brother's reputation is in the doghouse and she's just about to start her residency at the DPA. You know how important that is so why would you do anything to spoil it?"

She took a deep breath. He'd looked so angry a second ago.

But no wonder. She'd said something completely unforgiveable. She'd more or less accused him of being responsible for the smallpox outbreak. And he obviously wasn't.

Callum had already told her how difficult this would be for Sawyer. He was the one person here with more experience than her. Whether she liked it or not, she needed him. The last thing she should be doing was insulting him.

And more to the point, he was right. She hadn't told anyone about Isabel. She couldn't have dealt with the reaction that she'd been in a car crash that had killed her sister—a sister who would have given anything to work at the DPA. She hadn't let anyone in on her secret. Why should Violet?

She was telling herself to be reasonable and rational.

But something was skewing her thought processes. He had a sister. And it had caught her unawares.

It seemed ridiculous. Half the world had a sister. But most of the time she was prepared. She was ready. This time she hadn't been.

It didn't help that Violet Connelly was one of the sweetest people she knew. Not unlike Isabel. The fist squeezed around her heart even tighter.

She met his gaze. His face was flushed; he was still holding back his anger.

She'd kept her family secret too. She hadn't done anything to spoil her job at the DPA. She hadn't gone to her interview and said, *Well, actually, this was my sister Isabel's dream and since I was driving the car that killed her I feel I owe it to her.*

She took a deep breath, "I guess I wouldn't do anything to spoil it," she murmured.

He moved closer to her, the edges of his hair now wet around his face. "Our mum got remarried when I was a teenager. Violet was still quite young—she changed her name to our stepfather's. I didn't."

She raised her eyebrows at him. "What? You mean you were a rebellious teenager, Sawyer?" Anything to lighten the mood, anything to ease the tension in the room that was still bubbling away in her stomach. Anything to release the squeezing around her heart.

He nodded slowly. Then something else jarred into her mind.

"Does Evan Hunter know Violet's your sister?" She'd spoken to him numerous times on the phone today. "It was Evan that wanted you checked out."

He rolled his eyes. "I know that. Evan and I go way back. I haven't had a chance to phone Violet yet. I meant to, I just got caught up in everything. She's texted me and called me. She must have heard my name mentioned at the DPA. I need to fill her in on the details."

"You mean she didn't know you were here?" She couldn't keep the shock out of her voice. Why on earth would his sister not know where was?

He hesitated and for a second looked kind of sheepish. For a man with a reputation as a bad boy it almost didn't fit.

"I kind of dropped off the radar."

No. She didn't get this. She didn't get this at all.

"What do you mean? I know you didn't tell anyone at the DPA where you were—in a way, I almost kind of get that. But your sister? Your own sister, Matt?"

Her voice was raised. She couldn't help it. He had a sister. He had options. Options she didn't have.

How on earth could he do that? How long had he been off the radar? Six years?

Six years of no contact? It was unthinkable.

Her voice was shaking. "How could you do that, Matt? You have a sister who clearly loves you. She must have been frantic with worry. She's still frantic with worry. Why would you do that to her? Why would you put her through that?"

There it was again. That action. The one he always

did when he was thinking of an answer. He ran his fingers through his hair. "It's not as bad as it sounds."

She stepped right up to him. "Really? How? How is it not as bad as it sounds? Explain to me, Matt."

She was mad. She could never have done that. Never have cut Isabel out of her life for six years. It was unthinkable.

Nearly as unthinkable as being responsible for her own sister's death.

"I texted her. Not often. Just every now and then to let her know I was safe."

"And that was supposed to be good enough?"

He flung his hands up in frustration and shouted, "You don't know, Callie. You don't know anything. That was as much as I could manage. I needed time. I needed space. I didn't want anything familiar around me. I wanted to get my head straight."

"For six years?" She was shouting back.

His lips tightened. She knew there were tears threatening to spill down her cheeks. She couldn't help it. What a waste. He'd dared to risk his relationship with his sister.

A relationship she'd give anything to have again. It made her hate him.

"Not everything in life is part of a plan, Callie. Maybe if you get some life experience, you'll find that out."

She felt as if he'd just punched her in the ribs.

He couldn't be more wrong if he'd tried.

But, right now, in the middle of the night, she was hardly going to fill in the blanks to a man she hardly knew.

It was time to get some perspective. He had no idea

how much those words had hurt. And she'd no intention of telling him.

Distance. That's what she needed.

Being in an enclosed space with Matt Sawyer was doing weird things to her. Being in an enforced quarantine for up to eighteen days would plain drive her crazy.

"Sawyer!"

The shout came from down the corridor, followed by the sound of thudding feet. They both sprang to the door at once, yanking it open and spilling out into the hallway.

"What is it?"

The nurse was red faced, gasping for breath. "There you are. I need help. Jack's struggling to breathe—he needs to be intubated. The spots must be causing his airway to swell." She glanced from one to the other. "Tell me we've got a pediatrician who can do this?"

Their eyes met.

They didn't have pediatric intensive care facilities. They were an ER—not a PICU. Their options were limited.

Sawyer grabbed a gown and a mask. "I'll do it." He started to run down the corridor before she could ask any questions. "Get me a portable ventilator," he shouted over his shoulder.

Her head flooded with thoughts. What did the plan say? Were there algorithms for intubating smallpox patients? Were there risks attached to ventilating this child and possibly allowing the spread of disease?

There was no time to think. There was only time to act.

Sawyer had already sprung into action.

And for once she agreed.

CHAPTER FIVE

EVERYTHING HAPPENED IN a blur. A portable ventilator seemed to appear out of thin air.

The fear that had been hanging around everyone, crystallizing in the air, was pushed to one side.

Jack's stats were poor, his lips tinged with blue, but his face was red with the strain of struggling for breath.

Intubating a child was never easy. Particularly a child who was panicking. Sawyer was at the bedside in a flash. "Give me some sedation."

The nurse next to him nodded, pulled up the agreed dose and handed him the syringe.

Sawyer leant over Jack. The panic flaring behind the little boy's eyes was obvious. Sawyer tapped his arm at the point where Jack's cannula was sited. "I know you're having trouble, little man. But I'm going to help you sort that out. I'm going to give you something to make you a little sleepy then put a tube down your throat to help you breathe. It will make things much better."

On a normal day he would have given a child some time to ask questions. Then again, on a normal day he wouldn't be doing this. He administered the drug quickly, waiting for Jack's muscles to relax.

A few seconds later his little body sagged and the whole team moved seamlessly. Sawyer positioned himself at the head of the bed. "Give me a straight-blade laryngoscope and the smallest ET tube you've got."

Callie pulled the light closer, trying to aid him as he slid the tube into place. It didn't help that it was the middle of the night and there was no natural light. It would be tricky to intubate a partially blocked airway, not something that she would ever wish to attempt. It had been a long time since she'd been in an emergency situation like this. DPA callouts usually involved febrile kids and adults and lots of sick bowls and emergency commodes.

On occasion, people got really sick and died. But Callie didn't usually get involved in that side of things. She was usually left to consider the big picture—the spread of disease.

Watching a little kid struggle for breath was something else entirely.

She gave a sigh of relief as Sawyer slid the tube into place and attached the ventilator. There was a murmur between him and nurse standing at the bedside as they set the machine. Callie frowned. Who was she? She didn't recognize her.

In fact, she didn't recognize half the people in this room. Was this what happened in the case of a medical emergency? Isolation procedures were ignored?

She squeezed her eyes shut as she tried to rationalize her thoughts. Isolation procedures weren't being ignored. Everyone in here had the regulation disposable gowns, masks and gloves in place. But there was a whole host of new people in this room—not just the restricted one or two.

One of the residents was talking in a low voice to the parents, trying to calm them. Another nurse was standing next to the half-pulled curtain next to Ben. She was leaning over him, obviously trying to distract him from the events surrounding him, telling him a long-winded version of the latest kids' movie.

Another guy came through the door. "You wanted a pediatrician? You've got one."

Callie's head shot up. "Where on earth did you come from?"

She couldn't see his face properly behind his fitted mask but his eyes flitted over to her and then instantly away. His priority was obviously the child, not the surrounding bureaucracy. "Upstairs," he said, as he walked over to the bed and started to fire questions at Sawyer, who turned to face him.

"Wish you'd got here five minutes ago," he said.

Callie was incredulous. "*Upstairs?* What do you mean, upstairs? This unit is closed. There's no one going out and no one coming in." Her hands were on her hips.

She was watching her whole world disintegrate around her. The first rule of quarantine: no one in, no one out. "Which door did you come through? Who let you through? Didn't you realize there was a quarantine in force down here? Do you know you've put yourself at risk by walking into this room?"

She was shouting. She couldn't help it. Next she would have infected people running down the streets and the media crucifying the DPA for not handling the outbreak appropriately. Evan Hunter would be on the phone telling her she was a failure.

"Callie." It was Sawyer. He was right in front of her, his pale green eyes visible above the mask. "Calm down. We put out a call for a pediatrician. We can't handle these kids ourselves."

"You did what?" She couldn't believe it. This was the

problem with delegating. Mistakes got made. People did things they shouldn't. People did things that put others at risk. "Who gave you the right to do that?"

"I did." Sawyer's voice was calm but firm. "Decisions like this get made all the time. I'm in charge of the clinical care of these patients. And, as much as I don't like to admit it, this is getting beyond my level of expertise." He nodded towards the pediatrician. "Dan's great. We discussed the risks a little earlier. He knows he'll need to be vaccinated."

"It's much more than that!" She exploded. She couldn't help it. "Once he's vaccinated he may be able to look after these children but it'll put him out of commission for the general hospital for nearly a month. There's no way a doctor exposed to the smallpox virus through vaccination can be near anyone who is immuno-compromised. "Did you even think about that, Sawyer? Did you even consider it? And it's not just him. Who are all these people?" Her hand swept around the room. "They'll all need to be vaccinated too!"

"Stop it." She could sense his gritted teeth beneath the mask. He leaned closer, "You're making a scene and, quite frankly, it's not helping. Do you really think you're telling me anything I don't know or haven't already discussed with Dan? Do you really think these people don't already know the risks attached to coming into this room?"

She could feel the tiny hairs stand up at the back of her neck—and not in a good way. But he wasn't finished. "The difference between you and me, Callie, is that I know when I'm beaten. I know when to look for other options—options not in the plan. It's time you learned some new skills. Not everything in life is down in black and white."

He turned and walked away from her, leaving her stunned. She watched the second hand tick around on the clock on the wall in front of her. Less than twenty minutes ago she'd almost been in a compromising position with him.

Then, in the blink of an eye, everything had changed.

He made her want to cry. He made her want to scream. He was truly and utterly driving her crazy. The tears had automatically pooled at the corners of her eyes.

And it wasn't just the fact he behaved like an insubordinate teenager. It wasn't just that standing near to him made her hair stand on end or that sometimes there was wisdom in his words, even though they weren't in the plan.

It was the fact that in the midst of all that she just didn't know what she thought of him. She didn't know how to *feel* around him.

She was focused. She was precise. She followed the plan. Most of the time she'd helped develop the plan. And back in Atlanta these had seemed smart, comprehensive plans. Back in Atlanta they had seemed to cover every eventuality.

But they didn't cover the Sawyer element.

Not at all. They didn't cover the get-under-your-skin clause.

A smell drifted past her nostrils. What was that? She glanced at her watch—it was nearly five in the morning. Where had the time gone?

"Pizza," came the shout from down the corridor. She walked quickly along the hallway. She had to get out of there. She didn't have any pediatric skills and Dan clearly had things under control.

She also needed a chance to regroup.

Twenty pizza boxes were being descended on from every angle. It was like a plague of locusts. Someone was reading the tops of the boxes, shouting out what was in each one. "Hawaiian. Ham and cheese. Vegetarian." Arms appeared from everywhere, grabbing at the outstretched boxes. "Tuna and pineapple? Who on earth ordered that?"

A smile broke over her face. Alison had taken her responsibilities very seriously earlier when Callie had asked her to organize food for the patients and staff.

She'd asked what Callie's favorites were and so far she'd magicked up banana and toffee muffins and her favorite pizza. She pushed her way to the front. "That's mine." She held out her hand for the box.

The guy behind the desk wrinkled his nose in disgust. "Take it," he said as he moved on to the one underneath.

She smiled and drifted off with her pizza box. She'd learned early on as a junior doctor that ordering takeout was a whole new skill. Order something simple that everyone liked and you would never see it. Sweet and sour chicken, pepperoni pizza, chicken tikka masala, all would disappear in a blink of an eye. Order something a little out the ordinary and no one would touch it with a bargepole.

Tuna and pineapple pizza was an acquired taste. Isabel had sworn by spinach and anchovies. Even the thought sent a horrible tremor down her spine and made a smile dance across her face.

Sometimes the memories were good. Sometimes the memories were fun.

The typical teenage fights over clothes and boys had almost been blotted from her mind. The competition between them in medical school continued to hover around her. Isabel always had to be first to see their exam results. To see if she'd beaten Callie. But it had been a pretty even split. Both of them had excelled in different areas. Callie in planning, anatomy and bio-chemistry and Isabel in epidemiology, diagnostics and patient care. If things had gone to plan, they could have been a dynamite team.

Callie leaned back in her chair, her appetite leaving her abruptly. It always happened like this.

She was fine, she was focused. Then it would hit her again—what she'd lost. Just tumbling out of nowhere, like a granite rock permanently pressing on her chest.

The grief counselor had told her she'd get over it. It would just take time. But every year—particularly if there was an event that Isabel had especially enjoyed—it just seemed to shadow her all the more.

She turned her head to the right. The pile of paper-work about the type C containment building. The place that was currently having power issues. Would Isabel really have handled all this better? Would Isabel have been better organized than she was?

Would she handle Sawyer better than she was?

Her leg started to itch again and her hand automati-cally went to her scrub trousers and started scratching. She didn't have time for this. She didn't have time to be morose. She had a containment facility to sort out and there was no time like the present. Why should city hall officials get to sleep when she couldn't? She took a bite of her pizza and lifted the phone.

The children were as settled as they could be. The par-ents had been calmed, and in the end Dan had decided to give Ben some sedation too. Nothing about this situ-ation was ideal and the little guy had become hysterical when he'd realized there was a machine breathing for his brother.

Sawyer breathed a sigh of relief. His too-big scrub trousers seemed to have given up trying to stay in place, partly due to the missing elastic at the waist and partly due to being weighed down by the phone in his pocket.

What time was it in Atlanta? He looked at his watch and tried to count it out. But what did it matter? Violet had been trying to phone him for hours. Whether he liked it or not, it was time to call her back.

He lifted his hand. Then pressed it down again on the desk.

He couldn't remember the last time his hand had shaken like that.

Come on. This was easy. It was one phone call.

So, how come the voices in his head had to will him on?

He took another breath and lifted his hand again, trying to ignore the shake. His fingers slipped and he missed the buttons.

Darn it. What kind of a fool was he?

Three-year-old kids could dial a phone—why couldn't he?

Concentrate. Get this over with. It would only be a few minutes out of his life.

The first time would be the worst. Once he'd done it, the heavy weight pressing on his chest might finally lift and let him breathe again.

Stop thinking about it, you moron—just dial!

He pressed the buttons on the phone, praying it might automatically jump to voicemail.

He didn't even hear the first ring. "DPA. Can I help you?"

"Violet Connelly, please."

There was a few moments' silence as the call was connected. He resisted the huge temptation to hang up and hide.

Hang up and go and find a beer.

"Violet Connelly."

He could almost picture her in his mind, doing ten things at once with the phone perched between her shoulder and her ear. Even at this time in the morning she'd be multi-tasking.

"Hello?"

Patience had never been her strong suit.

"Hey, Violet." His voice cracked.

There was a loud crash. All he could imagine was that her chair had just landed on the floor. "Sawyer? Sawyer?"

He cringed, guilt flooding through him. The concern and anxiety in her voice was crystal clear. He should have texted her hours ago. Why hadn't he? Ten seconds. That's all it would have taken.

Scrub that. He should have phoned her six years ago. Not just send the odd random text from an occasional phone.

"Yeah, it's Sawyer."

Some not very ladylike words spilled down the phone. The concern had quickly been replaced by anger. "'Hey, Violet'? Is that the best you can do? Six years, Matt. *Six years!*"

"I know. I'm sorry but—"

"You're sorry? *You're sorry?* You've got to be joking. I've been trying to phone you for hours. *Hours.* You logged that call here hours ago, Matt. You must have known I would hear about it straight away. I've been trying to contact you ever since. I've been frantic."

"Violet, please—"

"Please? Please?" It was obvious she wasn't going to let him speak. Six years of worry and pent-up frustration were erupting all over him. "How do you think I feel? How do think it felt to know that after six years you phone the DPA and ask to speak to Callum Ferguson? *Callum Ferguson?* You must have known I would be here. You must have known the news would spread like wildfire. I don't care that it's about a smallpox outbreak. I don't care that it's the scariest outbreak we've ever dealt with. I want you to stop for five minutes and think about what that felt like for me."

Wow.

One thing was for sure, she'd been waiting to say that for a long time.

If Violet could see him now she would see that for the first time in years he was hanging his head in shame. "Give me a break, sis."

"*Give you a break?* Right now, I'd like to break every bone in your body."

Ouch. Harsh. And definitely not Violet's normal response. During the biggest potential outbreak in years, she'd just found her lost brother. She must be stressed up to her eyeballs. The added fact that no one knew he was her brother couldn't be helping—and she wasn't finished yet.

"Why haven't you answered my texts? Why haven't you answered my phone calls?" He could hear it now. The tiny waver in her voice. Violet never liked anyone to know when she was upset. He could almost picture the glimmer of tears in her eyes.

He sighed. "I've been busy, sis. I've got some really sick kids here." He leaned back against the wall, "Plus I've got an invasion of DPA faces that I'd hoped never to see again."

He stopped talking. He didn't need to say any more. Violet knew exactly how he felt about all this. He'd never actually said the words to her, but his sister knew him better than anyone.

"You can do this, Sawyer." Her voice was almost a whisper. A cheerleading call for him. After all this time she was still trying to instill confidence and strength into him.

She was the one person in the world who could chew him out one minute, then fight to the death for him a second later.

Family. He'd almost forgotten what it felt like.

"I'm just in the wrong place at the wrong time again, Violet. Story of my life."

Silence again. She realized the enormity of his words. The price he'd paid the last time had almost destroyed him.

"Are you safe? Did you put yourself at risk before you realized what it was?"

It was natural question—a sisterly question—but it still grated. Especially when he'd been part of the DPA. "I was in the same room as the kids, breathing the same air. I took precautions as soon as I had reason for concern, but they didn't have the appropriate masks. I had to send the other member of staff away— she's pregnant."

He heard Violet's sharp intake of breath. She knew exactly the impact that must have had on him.

"So, for a couple of hours it was just me treating the kids. You know how it is, Violet. That's the way it's got to be. I've had my smallpox vaccination. Now I just need to wait."

"I don't like this. I don't like any of this. I've waited months to hear from you again—eight measly texts in six years—and now this? All I've ever wanted to know is that you were safe, Sawyer, but when I finally hear from you, you're in the most dangerous place of all. It just doesn't seem real."

Sawyer felt himself bristle. He didn't want to get into this with Violet. He didn't want to answer a million questions about where he'd been or what he'd been doing. That was a conversation for another day—and maybe not even then.

And even though he could hear the note of desperation in her voice, he just couldn't go there.

"How's Callum? Have you heard if he's okay? I tried to call the hospital earlier, but they wouldn't tell me anything."

There was hesitation at the other end. She was obviously trying to decide what to tell him. "He's had a massive MI. They took him for angioplasty hours ago and apparently it went well."

There it was again. That tightening feeling around his chest. The way it always came when things were outside his control.

He hated the fact that even though he was a doctor he couldn't always help the people he loved.

He changed the subject.

"What do you know about Callie Turner? She seems a little out of her depth."

"You think?" Violet's answer was snappy, verging on indignant. She was obviously suffering from the same lack of sleep that he was. He was forgetting what time it was. "Callie's one of the best doctors I've worked with. She does everything to the letter. She's very focused, very ordered. Don't get in her way, Sawyer, she won't like it."

"Tell me something I don't know." In a way he was

surprised. Violet was always honest with him. She would tell him if she had any doubts about Callie. The fact that she hadn't mentioned even one was interesting. He decided to take a new tack. "What about her scars?"

"What scars? Callie has scars?"

She sounded genuinely surprised. Didn't the women in the DPA locker room look at each other? Maybe he should call them all on their observation skills.

"Yeah. A big one, snaking right down her leg. She didn't get it at work, then?"

"How come you've seen Callie's scars? Ah...the protective clothing. I get it. No, I had no idea Callie had a scar. She definitely didn't get it at work. She's never had any accidents here. It must be from years ago."

He leaned against the wall just outside the children's room again. All of a sudden he was embarrassed. He hadn't had a proper conversation with his sister in the last few years and he was asking her about other people? He should be ashamed of himself. He took a deep breath, "How are you, Violet? Are you okay?"

"How do you think I am? The biggest potential outbreak in who knows how long and, oh, yeah, my brother's in the middle of it. The DPA's in an uproar. Some rooms are deathly silent and in others you can't even hear yourself think. We've got another couple of outbreaks in other places but none like this." She lowered her voice, as if she was hiding her conversation from someone near her. "What do you think? Do you really think it's smallpox?"

He blew a stream of air out through his lips. "That's the million-dollar question. I'm sure it's a pox—and it definitely isn't chicken pox. But am I sure it's smallpox?" He shook his head. "I just don't know, sis. That's for the lab rats to tell us."

He heard her laugh at his affectionate name for his friends who worked down in the labs. "By the way, Frank says hello. He also cursed a little. He was just about to start his vacation when your lab samples arrived. He says you owe him and his wife a trip to Hawaii."

Memories started to come flooding back into Sawyer's mind. Memories he'd blocked out for a long time. He'd worked with Frank Palmer for six years. They were the same age and had got married around the same time. When Helen had died, he just hadn't been able to stay in touch. Everything was a permanent reminder.

Frank's wife Lucy was a petite, gorgeous blonde who had probably had her suitcase packed with a different bikini for every day of their vacation. She would have been *mad*.

Helen and Lucy had been good friends. They'd made plans together and enjoyed each other's company. Lucy had been heartbroken when Helen had died.

His heart gave a little squeeze. It wasn't just his sister he hadn't considered.

He hadn't considered other people. Other people who had been devastated by Helen's death. He'd been too busy focusing on his own grief to allow anyone else's to touch him.

"Tell Frank I'm sorry—no, tell Lucy I'm sorry." He hesitated for a second then asked, "Frank and Lucy—do they have any kids?"

It had been another of Helen and Lucy's grand plans, that they would all have kids at the same time. They'd always joked that their imaginary offspring could be prom king and queen together.

He heard Violet take a deep breath and her voice had a new edge to it, a harsher edge. "You've been away too long, Sawyer. Frank and Lucy lost their daughter last year to stillbirth. It was an extremely traumatic time—Lucy nearly died and had to have a hysterectomy. They can't have any more children."

He felt as if someone had just twisted a knife in his guts. For a few fleeting seconds he'd been jealous. Jealous that Frank still had Lucy. That he still had a future with his wife.

Violet's words sent chills across his body. It just showed you—you never knew. You never knew the minute when things could come crashing down all around you.

And now he was feeling something else. Disgust with himself. He hadn't been there to support his friends in their time of need. People who had reached out to him when he'd been at his lowest ebb.

It didn't matter that he'd walked away and ignored everyone. He could still remember every card, every phone call, every email, every handshake.

Helen would have been livid with him. He could almost hear her reading him the Riot Act.

Touching reality again was making him realize that her death hadn't affected only him. It had affected everyone around them.

Some of the contact tracers in the team could barely look at him today.

And it wasn't a reflection on them. It was a reflection on *him*.

They had no idea how he would react to them. How he would react if they brought up the past and expressed their sympathies about Helen—even after all this time

Violet cleared her throat at the end of the line and he snapped back to attention. "I take it you're still flying under the radar in there? They haven't made the connection between us?" he asked.

"No. No one knows." He heard her breathe a sigh of relief. "Or if anybody knows, they're not saying anything. Evan Hunter's walking around here like a bear with a sore head. I've spent the last few hours trying to avoid him. He didn't take it well that you're involved in this."

Sawyer couldn't help the smile that automatically spread across his face. "He'll get over it," he murmured. He looked at his watch. "Hate to say it, sis, but I need to go. I might have a chance to get my head down for a couple of hours. One of the pediatricians has just arrived to share the responsibility of the kids. We've just had to intubate one of them. This might be the only chance I get to sleep in a while."

"Okay, Sawyer. Stay safe and keep an eye on Callie. She has lots of good qualities. And keep your phone switched on. If I call and you don't answer…"

"I get it, sis. Keep your head down and stay out of Evan Hunter's way. He'll find something else to gripe about soon."

He stared at the phone as he heard her hang up, puzzled by her parting shot about Callie. It was almost like a little beacon, glowing orange in the dark sea. She knew exactly how to play him. Some things never changed.

CHAPTER SIX

VIOLET HAD ONLY just replaced the receiver when Evan Hunter came stomping across the room, shouting orders as he went. They might be an hour ahead of Chicago but hadn't anyone told him it was six o'clock in the morning and most of the staff had been up all night?

"Somebody get that man a coffee," she grumbled as she slid her chair under the desk and pulled up the screen she'd been reviewing. It was a distribution model of the potential spread of the smallpox virus. They'd started working on this while they had still been trying to determine if the passengers on the plane had been exposed or not.

"Violet! *Violet!*"

Rats. It was almost as if he had an internal radar and could hear her thoughts.

"What?" She turned to face him as he hovered above her, obviously irritated by her lack of instant response. "What's happened?"

"Where have you been? I've been looking for you?"

Darn it. She'd only ducked out for five minutes to speak to Matt. How on earth could he have known that?

There was only way to shut him up. "Ladies' room." She gave him a sarcastic smile. That was all the information he would need.

He scowled at her. "I need you to get some background on Matt Sawyer for me. Find out where he's been for the last six years. Find out how he managed to end up in an E.R. in Chicago."

She was stunned. It was the last thing she had been expecting. A few hours ago it had been a whole hullaballoo about a graph of the potential spread of smallpox. And, well, yes, she could almost understand it. That was just the kind of thing he wanted to appear instantly before his eyes. Stuff the grunt work. He practically expected people to work at the speed of light. It wouldn't be the first time she'd told him in no uncertain terms that data needed to be checked and rechecked, assimilated and analyzed beyond any shadow of a doubt.

But this? Asking her to investigate her own brother?

It was totally out of left field. A complete bolt from the blue.

Anyone else might have been intimidated by his stance, leaning over her. But Violet wasn't. She'd been this close to Evan before. About six months ago after a work night out.

The medic and her boss. Never a good idea.

Too bad she couldn't shift the inappropriate memories out of her head, which came up at the most inopportune moments.

"Violet? Did you hear me?"

She snapped back to attention. Back to reality. Sawyer and Evan Hunter had never got on. She'd no idea why and she didn't really care. Just as well she'd never told her boss that Sawyer was her brother.

She stared at him, unfazed by his annoyed face. Violet didn't do well on lack of sleep. It was the standing family joke that everyone should stay out of her way if she'd had a bad night on call as a resident. Her patience had just flown out of the window.

"Why on earth do you want me to check up on Sawyer? Shouldn't we be focusing on the real issue—the potential smallpox outbreak? I thought you wanted a complete rundown on the potential spread? That's what I've been working on for the last few hours and I'm not finished yet."

Evan leaned closer. "Don't you dare tell me what to do right now. I'm the team leader around here. I decide what happens. Sawyer is irresponsible and reckless. He's the last person we can trust. And a few hours ago he phoned in the biggest threat to this country's health in years. Am I suspicious? Absolutely I am! Now..." he pointed at the computer "...find out where he's been and what he's been doing. I want to know now!"

He swept into the office next to her, slamming the door behind him as if he could knock it from its hinges.

Violet sagged back down into her seat. She didn't need to do what he asked. She'd been doing it for the last six years and had found nothing. *Nada.*

Apart from a few cursory texts since his wife's funeral and his departure from the DPA, she knew nothing.

His texts had only ever told her that he was safe. Nothing else. Not where he was or what he was doing.

The hard fact was that if she wanted to know where Sawyer had been she would have to ask him. And right now she had a distribution model to finish.

She stared at the slammed door. Violet was used to prioritizing her own workload.

She set her jaw.

Evan Hunter could wait.

* * *

He watched the walls shake around the door he had just slammed. What on earth was wrong with him?

Evan felt sick. He had potentially one of the most well-publicized outbreaks in the DPA's history to handle and at the heart of it all was a man he hated. A man he didn't trust.

And he was taking it out on the people around him—he was taking it out on Violet.

The last thing he should be doing.

The press was all over this. The media room at the DPA was currently packed out, with the phones ringing constantly. He could handle stress. It wasn't the first time he'd handled a major outbreak.

What he couldn't handle were his reactions to Violet.

Those were the things he couldn't control.

He was going to have to do something about it—and fast.

"Callie, phone."

Callie looked up from where she was standing, talking to Sawyer. The plans for the containment facility were almost complete. The nurse dangled the phone from her hand. "It's the lab."

Callie and Sawyer moved in unison, diving for the phone at the same time.

Their hands clashed and Callie shot him a dirty look and shoved him out of her way. "Callie Turner."

"It's Evan."

She really couldn't face any niceties. Her brain could only fix on one thing—and from the expression on Sawyer's face he felt the same way.

"What is it? What has Frank found?" Sawyer flinched next to her at the sound of Frank's name. What was that all about? Frank had worked at the DPA for-ever. They must know each other.

She could hear the deep intake of breath at the end of the phone. "Electron microscopy revealed a brick-shaped virus. It's definitely an orthopox."

Callie felt her insides twist. She knew better than to say the next words. But she couldn't help it—it was automatic. "He's sure?"

Beside her she saw Sawyer drop his head into his hands. He knew exactly what was being said.

"He's sure."

She touched his arm and met his pale green eyes, giving him a silent nod. Sawyer let loose a string of expletives. The lab was only confirming what they'd all suspected. It was the first step in trying to classify the disease. It just made it all seem a little too real.

It was time to get down to business. "How long be-fore he can be more specific?"

"He's still running the PCR. You know how this is—we could have something for you in twenty-four hours or it could take up to seven days. Direct fluorescent antigen testing has ruled out varicella. Tell Sawyer he was right—it's definitely not chicken pox." She heard Evan sigh. Those words must have been painful for him. "Your next stage is the move to the containment type C facility. Are you ready for that?"

Callie looked at the whiteboard on the wall next to her. Every detail was clearly displayed. Her team was good. "The power company's just been in touch to let us know the power has been reconnected. We're just wait-ing to hear back from the chief of police about closing the highway and getting the police escort. Once that's in order we'll be ready to move."

"Keep me posted. I'll be in touch if we have any more news."

Callie stood in a daze for a few seconds, the phone dangling from her hand. She was trying to assimilate the information she'd just been given. A warm hand closed over hers and replaced the receiver.

They didn't speak. For once it seemed that their minds were working in unison.

Callie looked around at her bustling colleagues. Someone was going to have to tell them. Someone was going to have to confirm that this was a real and credible threat. It wasn't just a suspicion any more. They'd moved a stage beyond that now.

And it was her job.

Her job to ensure the safety of her team under these confirmed conditions.

Her job to keep the staff informed.

Her job to be responsible for the patients who were—most likely—infected with smallpox.

Her job to help prevent the spread of the disease.

It was almost overwhelming. Could she really do all this?

Sawyer was watching her. He could see the tiny flare of panic in her eyes. And as much as this was the worst possible news, he knew it was time to step up.

They were close together, low enough for their voices not to be heard.

"What exactly did Evan say?"

"It's definitely an orthopox." The anxiety in her voice was palpable. But a little smile appeared on her face. "And Evan said to tell you that you were right—it's definitely not chicken pox. They've ruled it out."

He pulled back a little. "Evan Hunter said that?"

She nodded. "I think he was more or less pushed into a corner on that one." Her eyes swept the room, trepidation returning to them. "I need to tell the team. We have to move to the containment facility."

If only she could see what he did. At times she had a little-girl look about her, as if she was about to be swept away by a tidal wave. As if the situation and events were totally out of her control. But these were tiny, fleeting glimmers that disappeared in an instant.

Then she would tilt her chin and act exactly the way she should. Just like she was doing now.

She was pushing aside her own fears and focusing on the details of the job. Just like a good doctor should.

They were close together again. Hiding away from the rest of the world. Her eyes were much bluer this close up. Last time they'd been like this had been in a darkened room and he hadn't really had a chance to appreciate her finer features.

She was lucky. No lines marring her complexion, only some dark circles under her eyes. Her gaze met his and her brow wrinkled. "Can I do this, Matt?"

Matt. Hardly anyone called him that. Just the way she said the word took him by surprise. He was so used to being called by his surname that it actually made him stop for a moment. He reached out and took her hand. She didn't flinch, didn't pull away. She just inched a little closer.

He saw the glimmer of fear register in her eyes. Her tongue peeked out and ran along her dry lips, moistening them and leaving them glistening.

He was fixated. He couldn't look away.

He bent down, his lips brushing the side of her cheek.

"Of course you can do this, Callie. This is what you trained for."

If he turned his head just slightly his lips would be on hers. It was the most inappropriate, most inopportune moment. But Sawyer didn't care.

For the first time in a long time he was finally starting to feel again.

And everything else just paled in comparison.

He was getting another waft of that raspberry shampoo.

But then she moved, lowering her face beneath his and resting her hands on his shoulders. There was something else in her expression. It was almost as if she was taking a minute—as if she wanted to tell him something. And it was clear she had no idea about the thoughts currently circulating in his head.

He tried to focus. To take his gaze off her pink lips. She was close enough that he could smell the mints she'd been eating.

They couldn't stay like this. Any minute now someone in the E.R. would notice they were closer than normal.

He had to get some perspective before he did something he might regret.

He jerked back. "How long until we find out the diagnosis?"

If she noticed him pulling away she didn't react. "Evan wasn't sure. Anything from between another twenty-four hours up to seven days. But at the moment we still need to tell everyone the quarantine will last for seventeen days."

"Seven days is a long time to wait for a diagnosis."

She nodded and turned away from him. Focusing on work, getting back to the job. Staring up at the whiteboard. "I guess we'd better start vaccinating again. Everyone going to the type C unit needs to be vaccinated beforehand."

She was right. She was being professional. Her mind was focused on the job. Just where his should be.

He nodded and said the words he was supposed to. "Let's get to work."

How on earth was he going to manage in an enclosed space with her for the next seventeen days?

CHAPTER SEVEN

"Wow! How did they manage this in such a short space of time?"

Callie peered out of the transport-vehicle window as they approached the containment facility. It was more than impressive. A bright white building sitting in the middle of an industrial site.

It was almost the regulations personified.

A single building located at least one hundred yards from any other occupied facility. Non-shared air-conditioning, heating and adequate ventilation systems. Single rooms with negative air pressure. Advanced medical and laboratory systems. Dependable communication systems and controllable access.

Then, more than the obligatory one hundred yards away, another type R facility to host everyone who'd been exposed, vaccinated and hadn't developed any symptoms. All the patients who'd been exposed in the E.R. could now be safely housed and monitored for the next two weeks.

Sawyer pressed his face up against the window next to her. The slow-moving convoy had taken nearly forty minutes to get here. It had been a surreal experience. But, then again, it had been years since anything like this had happened. The fact that the ambulance transport crews were kitted out in masks, gloves, gowns and shoe covers probably hadn't helped. Particularly with the amount of news crews that surrounded the hospital.

Callie found that incredible. Who, in their right mind, news crews or not, would want to be that close to a possible smallpox outbreak? If she'd been any other kind of doctor she would have headed to the city limits as quickly as she could.

Callie shuddered at the thought of the news headlines that evening. The pictures of the crew transporting the 'infected' patients could be terrifying to the general public. She could only hope that Evan Hunter would be in charge of damage control.

"I guess it must have been something else. A school? Some kind of lab? A warehouse?" Sawyer wrinkled his nose, as if he was aware that none of those things really fitted. "Did Callum leave you any notes?"

Callie rummaged through the pile of papers on her lap. "I've been so busy sorting out the problems—getting the electricity and water turned on, medical supplies delivered—that I didn't really think about it. He just told me he'd identified 'suitable premises.' Ah, here it is." She dragged a pale cream piece of paper from the bottom of the pile.

"What's wrong?"

Her eyes were still scanning the page and what she was reading was obviously translating straight to her face. "It's just a little odd." She lifted her head and stared at the building again, "It was a research facility."

"What's odd about that?"

"It's apparently been here for the last hundred years." A strange sensation swept over her. "Do you think they used it for the last smallpox outbreak?"

"Now, there's a creepy thought."

They pulled up outside the buildings and both heads turned to look again. Sawyer opened the door and jumped down, holding out his hand to help Callie. She left her papers on her seat and jumped out with him.

They stood next to each other, hands on their hips, trying to work out what was going on. "It looks brand-new," Callie muttered.

"It certainly does. Maybe it's just had a coat of paint?"

He stepped forward and touched the exterior wall. "It's certainly had new windows and doors."

Callie nodded. "And a new ventilation system." She gave a nod to the system that was clearly venting all its air outside through the designated HEPA filters. "They couldn't possibly have had that last time round. It must have been used recently."

She turned around as the rest of the transport started to pull up behind them. "Let's take a look inside."

Sawyer matched her step for step as they strode through the building. Everything about it was perfect. A laboratory, newly refurbished patient rooms and clinical treatment rooms. Then a whole separate building that fitted with type R requirements, with single bedrooms and bathrooms where all the people under the containment could be housed, with extra facilities available for them all. Kitchens, sitting rooms, children's playrooms, even a cinema room, it was extraordinary.

All with the proper ventilation systems to prevent the spread of infection.

Callie ran her fingers along the wall in the one of the corridors. She didn't feel uneasy. This place didn't have a bad feeling attached to it, but there was a certain air of mystery. "If these walls could talk, what would they tell us?"

Sawyer turned to face her, "What do you mean?"

She pointed to the nearest room. "This almost seems too good to be true. This place has obviously been in use recently—though we did have to get the water and electricity switched back on. They haven't managed to do all this in twenty-four hours. I wonder what kind of research they did here?"

Sawyer pushed open the nearest room—full of state-of-the-art monitoring and ventilation equipment. "Does it really matter? We've got good facilities here." He nodded as Dan, the pediatrician, appeared at his back, entering the room to make sure it had everything he needed for the children.

A smile appeared across Dan's face. "These are the latest ventilators. I've been trying to get Chicago General to buy some. They cost serious money. They'll be perfect for the kids. But here's hoping I only need one." He gave a nod to Callie. "I don't know how you managed it but this is perfect."

That strange feeling spread again. "I don't know how I managed it either," she said quietly. Everything seemed to have miraculously fallen into place. Maybe her rant at Evan Hunter had worked. Someone in the DPA had excelled themselves here.

Sawyer placed a hand on Dan's shoulder. "How do you want to set things up? Do you want to have Jack and Ben in separate rooms? We've got the negative air pressure facilities here, we can use them."

He was obviously just trying to give Dan his place. As the only pediatrician, the care and responsibility of the two boys fell to him. It didn't make sense to bring in any other doctors. And although he wasn't a pediatrician Sawyer had already volunteered to assist with the care of Jack and Ben. Since he'd done the initial diagnosis he seemed reluctant to let them go. But he was quite happy to take instructions from Dan.

Dan shook his head. "Actually, no, I want to keep them together. They've been equally exposed anyway. Separating them at this time isn't going to benefit either of them. Unless you can tell me something different?"

Callie shook her head.

Sawyer cut in. "I'm with you, Dan. In that case, for the sake of the two of them, it's better they stay together. This place would be terrifying for a six- or seven-year-old on their own. There is no viable clinical or psychological reason to keep them apart. They're brothers. They're meant to be together. Let's not add to the stress."

Callie could feel her heart flutter in her chest. He couldn't possibly know or understand what those words would mean to her. It was just the fact that somebody, somewhere had even the slightest inkling about the connection between siblings. The reassurance of being together, no matter how unscientific. And the possible benefits for the boys.

She'd heard miraculous stories before about premature twins being reunited in the same special-care cot and the baby that had been expected to die had made an unlikely recovery.

She herself had been badly injured in the car accident, almost unconscious. But when it had become apparent that Isabel was going to die, an experienced nurse had insisted her trolley be pulled in next to her sister's. Then she'd lifted Isabel's hand to let Callie hold it as her sister's life had slipped away.

It had been the worst moment in Callie's life. If she hadn't been going straight to Theatre, they would have had to sedate her.

But now, with the benefit of hindsight, it was one of her most precious and treasured memories. She'd been able to say things to Isabel that she might never otherwise have had the chance to say. Even though she realized Isabel had probably not heard her, it had still given her comfort. It had also meant the world to her parents, who hadn't been able to make it to the hospital in time to see their daughter before she'd died.

So Sawyer's words and understanding meant more to her than she could ever possibly reveal.

Dan and Sawyer were already striding down the corridor, organizing the transfers from the ambulances. Staff were streaming past, carrying boxes that were systematically being unpacked into cupboards.

Callie walked back out and watched the rest of the people being shown into the other building, carrying their belongings with them. One of the planners came up and handed her a large plan of the building, complete with names assigned to every room. "Thought you'd need this, Callie."

She nodded as she looked over the plan, a smile crossing her face when she assimilated the sleeping arrangements. "We don't seem to have adequate laundry facilities." She lifted her head to the planner, who consulted his list and shook his head. "We need to get right on that. In the case of smallpox, laundry can be a risk. It can carry contaminated fluids. We need to make arrangements for the laundry to be put in biohazard bags and autoclaved." The planner scribbled furiously then walked away.

She felt Sawyer's hand on her shoulder. "Our home for the next, what, seventeen days?"

"Sixteen," she said firmly. "We've already done the

first day." She gave a little smile. "Think you can stand me for that long?"

"I might be forced to give you a haircut."

"Ditto."

He jerked back a little. "Isn't that some crazy quote from a romance movie?"

"I don't know. I don't watch romance movies. I'm more an action girl myself."

"Really?" There was distinct tone of disbelief in his voice.

"Yeah."

He shook his head. "Just when I think I know you, even a little, you say something to surprise me."

"That I like action movies? If that surprises you, you've led a pretty sheltered life." She realized the stupidity of her words as soon as they left her mouth. But it was too late. They were out there.

Sawyer didn't react. He just pulled out some equipment from the back of one of the ambulances and gave her a weak smile on the way past.

She was cringing inside. A man whose wife had died on a DPA mission had obviously never led a sheltered life. How could she possibly last another sixteen days around him without making an idiot of herself?

He turned back to face her, his expression unreadable. "What about Alison? Did everything work out okay?"

So it was back to business. A few seconds of personal chat that she'd just ruined. She'd only herself to blame. She forced a smile onto her face. "I think in a few hours we'll all wish we were Alison."

"How come?"

"We couldn't bring her here because we couldn't vaccinate her. The next option in the plan is to isolate the person at home. But Alison didn't want to take the risk of being isolated at home in case she put her family at risk."

Sawyer nodded. He would know that being isolated at home would be the logical answer but not entirely practical. "So you had to think outside the plan? Interesting." He folded his arms across his chest. "I bet that gave you a spasm. So what's happened to her?" The grin that had vanished a few minutes ago had reappeared. Callie resisted the temptation of rising to the bait.

"It seems that somebody in the DPA budget office was in a nice mood. They've rented out an entire boutique hotel for the next fortnight until we're sure she's symptom-free. Alison will be living in the lap of luxury."

Sawyer's response was instant. He shook his head. "Maybe to you or me. But not to her. Alison dotes on her kids. It will drive her crazy not to be with them for two weeks."

Callie tried not to grimace. She'd been thinking of the gorgeous surroundings, fabulous food, luxurious bedding and unlimited TV channels. She really hadn't thought much past the idea of ordering room service every night.

"I guess not," she murmured, as she followed him down the corridor as he dumped some more supplies in the treatment room.

"Let's grab our stuff and dump it in our rooms." They walked back outside and Sawyer lifted her rucksack and suit carrier from one of the vans. "Did you really travel this light? Or do you have a giant suitcase hidden somewhere?"

She laughed. "I do have a suitcase, but it's a carry-on." She looked around her, "I've no idea where it is, though. What about you?"

Sawyer lifted a polythene bag. "My worldly goods."

"You're joking, right?"

He shook his head. "I came to work to do a twelve-hour shift. I didn't realize I should have packed for a fortnight."

"Wow. We're really going to have to get you some clothes, aren't we?" She started to laugh. "What about all your hair products? Won't they need a suitcase all of their own?"

"Cheeky!" She ducked as he flung his bag at her head. The contents spilled on the ground. Another pair of Converses, a T-shirt, a pair of ripped jeans, a pair of boxers and a bunched up pair of socks. She raised her eyebrows as she stuffed the contents back in the bag and lifted up one shoe. "Two pairs?"

He shrugged. "That's the good pair. The scruffy ones are work shoes." She smiled at the kicked-in shoes she held in her hands. She wouldn't even have worn them to paint a fence—and these were the good ones. "Nothing else?"

"What? I wear scrubs at work all day. What else do I need?"

"I hate to think. You got anything to sleep in?"

"What kind of a question is that?"

"The kind of question from a woman who's sharing an apartment space, kitchen and bathroom with you."

Ever since she'd looked at the plan she'd felt nervous. Excited nervous, not scared nervous. Wondering what his reaction would be to the sleeping arrangements.

"Why aren't I sharing with Dan? Wouldn't that have made more sense?"

She nodded as they headed over to the building. "It

does—and he's sharing with us too, along with one of the other DPA doctors. Four people per apartment. But I guess they figured you'd be doing the opposite shifts from Dan. Doesn't make sense for you to be working at the same time."

"Callie, Sawyer!"

They turned their heads as one of the nurses shouted over to them.

"We need you in the treatment facility. There's a few patients with symptoms that need checking out."

They looked at each other and swiftly dumped their bags at the entrance.

"Guess we can do this later," Callie said flatly.

His gaze met hers. "I guess we can."

There was something in the way he said it. The tone of his voice. The way his eyes held contact with hers. The way there was a hint of smile on his face. It sent a weird tingle down her spine.

All of a sudden that excited nervousness didn't seem so odd after all.

Callie looked down at her map as they walked along the corridor. "Next left," she said.

It was late and they were both tired. Checking over a few symptoms had taken a lot longer than expected.

Sawyer pushed open the plain white door with the number seven on the front. It opened into a large sitting room with white walls and red carpet and a sofa. It was much bigger than she'd expected. An open-plan kitchen stood at one end of the room with a door to another corridor at the bottom.

Callie was a little shocked. It was much better than she had expected. "I thought it would be like student accommodation." She gave a little shrug, "You know, kind of drab and definitely tiny." She pressed her hand down on the comfortable sofa with matching cushions. "I guess not. Who do you think stayed here?"

"Who cares?" Sawyer had made his way to the pristine white kitchen and started to rummage through a cardboard box sitting on one of the worktops. "Wonder where this came from? Gotta love those planners. I'm starving." He emptied the contents onto the surface—milk, bread, butter, cereal. Callie automatically opened the door to the fridge and started depositing the perishable items inside.

"Yes!" He punched his hand in the air as if he'd just won an award.

"What is it?"

"My favorites." He pulled out a packet of chocolate cookies and ripped it open. "I didn't realize how hungry I was." He tilted his head at her as the cookie disappeared in two bites. "Who sorted all this stuff out? Was it Alison?" He looked back in the box. "Because I swear, if I find a tuna pizza in here I'll—"

"You'll what?" She swatted his arm. She almost felt relieved. He was back to his relaxed self again. The way she preferred him. The way he was when he didn't feel as if he had the weight of the world on his shoulders. Along with two very sick kids.

He squinted. "It's a bit bright in here, isn't it?"

Her eyes swept around the unexplored apartment again. It was clear neither of their other colleagues had found their way here yet. She nodded and flicked the overhead light back off, plunging them back into darkness. She walked over and pulled the curtain at the window, which looked onto the rest of the industrial site. Dim light flooded through the kitchen. The moon was high in the dark sky outside and the external lights surrounding the buildings let a little more light into the room.

It was nice. Kind of private.

Sawyer flicked the switch on the kettle. "A coffee pot and some decent beans obviously weren't on the inventory."

"And that'll be my fault, will it?" In the dim light Sawyer didn't seem anywhere as near as intimidating as before.

Maybe that was what he needed. To be out of the hospital environment and the things he was obviously struggling with. Maybe this—an environment like someone's home—made him feel more chilled. More easy to be around.

Or maybe she was remembering the last time they'd been in a darkened room together. Because she was feeling herself drawn towards him, her feet on autopilot.

She was up close, just under his chin. He turned back round and gave a little start at her close proximity. Was she reading this all wrong?

But from the lazy smile that came across his face she obviously wasn't.

He leaned one elbow on the counter top. "Did I say it was your fault?" He was so close that his breath warmed her cheeks.

"You didn't have to, but it always seems that way."

He lifted his hand and rested it gently on her hip. "Maybe you're just a little too uptight. Maybe you need to stop following the rule book all the time." He moved forward in the darkness, his lips brushing against her ear. "Maybe—just maybe—you need to learn to relax a little."

It was the way he said it. His tone of voice. She hadn't read anything wrong.

She was reading everything perfectly. He thought she couldn't throw the rule book away? Even for a second?

Under normal circumstances she would have been horrified. But nothing about this was normal. And nothing about how she felt drawn to this man was normal.

Maybe for just five minutes she could follow her own rules. Not the ones that felt safe.

She looked at him steadily in the dim light. "Maybe. I was just thinking the same thing about you. Maybe you need to learn to relax too," she whispered.

For a second nothing happened. Her breath felt caught in her chest. Her skin prickled. What would he do?

It was almost as if she could see him thinking, weighing up things in his mind. Had she just made a huge mistake? The wait was killing her.

Then she felt it—a warm hand slipping into hers. It electrified her skin. He pulled her over towards the sofa and sat. He tugged her down next to him, the moonlight spilling over them both.

Maybe she should feel a little intimidated by how close they were. If she leaned forward right now she could brush her nose against his. But she didn't feel intimidated at all. She didn't feel they were close enough.

In the dim moonlight and up this close she had her best-ever view of his pale green eyes. She'd seen a previous stone that color once in a tiny boutique jeweler. It was called paraiba tourmaline and she'd never seen one again. Which was a pity because it was the exact color of his eyes. And she could see the little lines all around the corners of his eyes. Were they laughter lines? Or were they from the permanent frown that he usually saved for her?

His shaggy brown hair didn't annoy her nearly so

much when she had a close-up view. She kind of liked it. In fact, for a split second she could see her fingers running through it in the midst of…

She shook that thought from her mind, squeezing her eyes shut for a second. *Wow. Where had that come from?*

But she didn't feel embarrassed. She didn't feel awkward. The heat emanating from his body was warming hers. And she was enjoying it. No matter how crazy that was.

When had been the last time she'd been in this position? This close to a man? It must have been over a year ago.

Harry. Like all the others, he hadn't worked out either. It wasn't that there had been anything wrong with him. He had been kind, handsome, considerate. Just what any girl would want. But she just hadn't connected with him. Hadn't been able to let herself go enough to plan ahead for a future with him in it. Because that would have meant letting him in. Telling him everything he'd needed to know. And she hadn't been there yet.

She hadn't been ready to share.

So what was so different about Sawyer?

Was it that he challenged her to let the rule book go? Was it that he pushed her to do better?

Or was it that he'd lived through the pain of loss himself? Maybe he would understand in a way that no one else could? Maybe that was the truth of why she was drawn to him—a fellow lost soul.

He moved. The shadows had gone from his eyes and there was no barrier between them—no shutters.

Callie's stomach was in a little knot. Was he finally

letting down his guard? Would he actually talk to her about what had happened?

His hand came down on her the side of her leg. His warm hand instantly connected, shooting warmth through her thin scrub trousers.

"So, Callie, are you going to tell me?"

She turned to face him. His hand was still on her leg but now she'd angled her body around to face his so they were almost nose to nose.

"About what happened. To your leg."

This was it the moment she should pull away. The time for her to retreat into herself and hide away from the rest of the world.

She'd done it before. It was automatic. It was so easy.

Her hands moved, up around his neck.

She was about to take the biggest step she'd ever taken.

"Not now. Maybe later."

Four words. That was all.

But it felt like a giant leap forward.

It was the first time she'd ever even considered telling someone about what had happened.

He could never know the strength that had taken.

She was sure she started to hold her breath. She believe how distracted she was right now. She was sure he must think her a little crazy.

But she didn't have time to think of any of these things.

Because she was kissing Sawyer.

CHAPTER EIGHT

CALLIE WASN'T QUITE sure who made the first move. She didn't think it was her, but then again she didn't think it was him. It was almost as if they read each other's minds and moved simultaneously.

There was no light-hearted kissing. No nibbling. Nothing gentle. Nothing delicate.

From the second their lips locked there were no holds barred. His lips devoured hers, fully, passionately without a moment's hesitation. And she liked it.

She could feel the scrape of his emerging bristles on his chin against her skin, abrading it as they kissed. Their teeth clashed and they both ignored it, his hand pressing firmly on her back to bring her even closer.

She wanted to run her hands over his body, across his chest and down his back. Everything about her was acting on instinct. The one thing she wasn't used to.

His kisses moved. Down her neck, along her throat. Then he groaned and shifted position, pushing her onto her back on the sofa and slowly moving on top of her. He pressed her arms above her head, straddling her body, and starting work on her neck again.

She was gasping now, willing him to go lower. Itching to let her hands feel his skin under her palms.

She wrenched one of her hands free and grabbed

hold of his hair, pulling his head back up towards her and capturing his lips again. She loved the feel of them. She loved the way he kissed her.

If this was what kissing a bad boy was like, she should have done it years ago.

She moved her head, kissing down his neck and releasing her other hand to slide it around his back. She was pulling him closer, working her hands under his scrub top, dancing her fingers up and down his spine.

She heard him groan and felt his muscles flex beneath her fingers. Somehow knowing she had some control made her feel bolder. She wanted to feel his skin against hers, she wanted to *see* his skin. She pulled at his scrub top, tugging it upwards until he'd no choice but to stop kissing her for a second and pull it over his head.

There. Just what she wanted. Sawyer, bare-chested.

She ran her fingers across the scattered dark hairs on his chest, wishing they were tickling her bare skin. But he hadn't moved quite as quickly as she had. His fingers were just edging beneath her top. Her back arched automatically towards him, willing him on.

He gave her that lazy smile. *Did this man know just how sexy he was?* Then he bent and whispered in her ear. "Have a little patience, Callie."

Patience. The last thing on her mind right now.

His voice was rugged, husky. A perfect voice for the middle of the night in a darkened room in a place that belonged to neither of them. It seemed all the more wicked. All the more illicit.

He started tugging her top over her head. His eyes widened at the pink satin push-up bra he revealed. Callie was a girl who loved her fancy matching underwear, no matter what clothes she was wearing on top. *Thank heavens for small mercies.* Just wait until he reached the thong.

He didn't hesitate for a second. His gaze was fixed on her breasts enclosed in the pink satin. "So you have a thing for pale colors and matching sets? Last time I saw you half-dressed it was in lilac."

His voice was lower. Growling. And it turned her on a lot. "I have lots of matching sets." She raised her eyebrows and gave him a calculating smile. "What's your favorite color?"

"Red," he groaned, as his palms skirted the outside of the bra cups. Her breasts seemed to be swelling at his touch. But the appreciation of her underwear was momentary. Sawyer cut to the chase—his patience obviously as limited as hers. He reached behind her back and released the clasp, her bra flung aside a moment later, releasing her breasts into his clutches. As his teeth brushed against her peaked nipple she could begin to feel the throb between her legs.

"Or maybe emerald green." He tweaked, licked and blew his hot breath across her as she moaned beneath him. Her hands kept trying to move, to make further contact with his skin, to get between them and reach down below. But he kept moving, changing position and diverting her attention.

This man had talent in the diverting attention stakes.

Her legs automatically widened and he moved from straddling her to bringing his legs between her thighs. Again she acted on instinct, raising her hips and tilting her pelvis towards him. Thin scrub trousers couldn't disguise what lay beneath and she gave a little gasp.

His hand slid beneath her scrub trousers, sliding first across her pelvis then down along her thigh, his fingers tracing the line of her scar. But she didn't flinch, she didn't jerk the way she had when some other lover had touched it. This felt easy, this felt natural. His hand ran back up the inside of her leg, sending a rush of blood to her groin, working his way around her buttocks and smiling as he played with her thong. He gave a little tug and there was an instant ping, along with a loosening sensation. Thirty dollars gone in one tug. She could almost visualize the thin gossamer straps breaking. It only excited her more.

His fingers crept back around to the front, coming into contact with her pubic curls. She moaned and opened her legs, willing his fingers closer, and her frustration built.

The scrub trousers were annoying her now. She didn't want any barrier between them. She didn't want anything between them at all. She moved his arms out of the way to give her a clear path to where she wanted to go.

She pushed her hand down the front of his scrub trousers, ignoring his boxers and sliding right inside. She could feel his back arch and she wrapped her hand around him. Finally. Just what she wanted.

His mouth was moving lower now, his fingers still dancing a fine tune as she moaned in response. This bad boy certainly knew how to play her.

"Anyone home?" The door of the apartment slammed loudly.

They froze. For a few seconds neither of them moved.

Dan. It was Dan. The bright light flicked on, sending illumination over their bare skin. Sending them both into instant panic.

Sawyer pushed himself up, pulling his hand out of Callie's scrub trousers and starting to stand. Callie's head jerked from side to side, trying to find where Sawyer had flung her bra.

That was as far as they got.

Dan had obviously walked the few steps into the apartment and his jaw dropped.

Callie could have died.

She didn't even have time to cover her breasts—her scrub top had been flung far behind in her in the midst of passion. Sawyer let out an expletive and stepped in front of her. "Give us a second, will you, Dan?"

Dan gulped. "Sure." The color spread rapidly up his cheeks as he walked back outside in stunned silence.

Sawyer closed the apartment door and leaned against it.

Callie felt the tears rapidly building in her eyes. She wanted to die of embarrassment. She felt like some teenager caught in a compromising position.

The silence in the room was deafening. She moved quickly, threading her arms back through her bra, fastening it and pulling the crumpled scrub top over her head.

Dan's face was haunting her. He'd seen her almost naked. A guy she hardly knew.

Sawyer was still standing with his back against the door, his eyes not meeting hers. The obvious bulge was still apparent in his thin scrub trousers. And the irony of it hit her. *Another guy she hardly knew.*

This wasn't her. She didn't act like this. She sometimes didn't even kiss on the first date.

But Sawyer had literally been by her side since she'd arrived in Chicago and the attraction had been instant. Instant but ignored.

This was the worse possible time for her. She needed to be a leader—someone that people could respect and respond to. What if Dan told the others what he'd just seen? That the doctor in charge of the potential small-pox outbreak had been lying half-naked on the sofa with a guy she'd just met?

What if he told them that her mind certainly wasn't on the job? That she was focusing on something else entirely?

She squeezed her eyes shut and tried to push the horrible thoughts from her mind. Could this be any worse?

Yes, it could.

Sawyer still couldn't look her in the eye. He hadn't even moved to pull his scrub top back on. He was just leaning against the door, his eyes fixed on the window straight ahead.

What was worse than getting caught in a compromising position with the bad boy?

Getting ignored by the man who'd just kissed you as if his life depended on it.

"Are you ready?" His voice startled her. It was almost a growl. Almost as if he thought this was all her fault.

It made her bristle. It made her defensive. It hurt.

She had to work with this man. She had to *live* with this man for the next two weeks. It would be so easy to hide her scarlet cheeks, put her head down and walk out of this room. But she couldn't. Not like this.

"I'll be ready to go when you can look me in the eye, Matt."

His head shot up. He flinched. It was so unfair that he was still standing there, bare-chested, right before her eyes. Men had it easy. He looked startled by the use of his first name—she'd only ever called him that a few times.

Or was he just surprised she'd immediately called him on his reaction?

"Let's not get into this now." He turned his back on her, picked up his scrub top, clenching it in his fingers, and put his hand on the door.

"Why not?" She couldn't think straight. Not after what had just happened.

"What?" He was beginning to look annoyed.

"Why not get into it now?" She gestured towards the door. "I'm really not looking forward to going out there and facing Dan. I don't even want to think about how I'm going to have to appeal to his better nature not to tell everyone about this." She shook her head. "My guess is that the last thing he'll want to do is share an apartment with us. Who would? We've just behaved like a pair of hormone-crazed teenagers."

She stepped forward and put her hand on his chest and he visibly flinched again. *Actions spoke louder than words.* It told her everything she needed to know.

"We have to work together, Matt. We've been stuck together in close proximity, under pressure, for the last two days. I guess we're just going to have to chalk this up to experience."

Her heart was thudding against her chest. She had no idea if she'd just played him right. She was trying to remain detached. She was trying to be rational. But she didn't feel that way.

In truth, she was mortified.

Hot and heavy after a first kiss, after only a couple of days.

She didn't need to justify herself. She didn't need to explain herself. But she just couldn't let him think that was her normal behavior.

"I guess there's a first time for everything." She kept her voice as steady as she could. He'd finally raised his eyes to meet hers but the shutters were well and truly down again. "It's probably best for both our sakes, and for the people we're responsible for, that there isn't a repeat performance."

His face remained blank. As if he was listening to her words but not really hearing them.

"If you will let me pass, I'll go and face the music with Dan."

He stepped out of her way, remaining silent.

She opened the door and stepped out into the corridor. His silence was angering her now. First he wouldn't look at her. Now he wasn't talking to her.

She turned her head to the side, praying he wouldn't see the tears glistening in her eyes. "Maybe you'd better try and sort out other sleeping arrangements. This situation is untenable."

On the outside Sawyer was frozen to the spot, but on the inside he was a bubbling cauldron, full of sulfur and about to explode.

Dan had appeared at the worst possible time—that much was obvious.

And Callie was right. They both had to pray that he would keep things to himself; otherwise Callie's authority could disappear in the blink of an eye. And in a situation like this that could be disastrous.

He knew that she'd been hurt by his lack of response but the truth was that she was right, he couldn't look her in the eye. And after what they'd just shared Callie would have wanted some kind of sign. A sign as to whether this had been just a one-off mistake or if it could lead somewhere.

And the truth was he just didn't know.

Every nerve ending in his body was on fire. Every place that she'd touched his skin seemed to burn. She'd been so willing, so responsive. If Dan hadn't appeared, chances were nothing would have stopped them.

And how would he have felt then?

Feel.

That was the problem.

Sawyer had been down this road before. Meet a woman in a bar, exchange small talk, have meaningless sex, sneak out before morning.

But all of a sudden the road had changed direction.

No, scrap that, this was an entirely new road.

In the space of a couple of days this woman had started to get under his skin. To invade his senses. To make him feel things that he hadn't felt since he'd first met Helen.

And it felt like a betrayal. It didn't matter that Helen had been dead for six years. It didn't matter that she would have never have wanted him to lead this closed-off life. His impersonation of the walking dead was growing stale, even for him.

But on any of his chance encounters before, he'd never *felt* anything. Apart from the obvious. He'd just been going through the motions. Making sure everything still worked.

This was different. This was nothing like that.

From the moment Callie Turner had appeared on his radar everything had turned upside down.

At first he'd thought he was annoyed because Callum was sick, then he'd thought it was because she was inexperienced. Or struggling. Or getting things wrong. Or all of the above.

But the truth was he was looking for a reason—any reason—not to like Callie Turner.

He was fighting the way he was drawn to her—was curious about her and wanted to know more.

The sight of her getting changed into her scrubs. The scar on her leg. The almost kiss in the treatment room.

The way he'd felt as soon as his lips had touched hers. The way she'd reacted to his touch. The feel of her skin next to his. The arch of her back. The tilt of her pelvis. The small groan she'd made at the back of her throat.

All of it driving him crazy. All of it making him act on instinct. Something he hadn't allowed to happen in a long time.

How could he have gotten into this? How could he have ended up in a specialist containment unit for a seemingly extinct disease? All of this was so unreal. This had bad movie written all over it.

Wrong place, wrong time.

The words danced around his brain again. He'd first thought them when he'd raised the alarm about the apparent smallpox cases. The words had been so in tune with how he had been feeling. He couldn't wait to get out of Chicago General. He couldn't wait to get away from the whole situation.

But now the words made him feel uncomfortable. He still didn't want to do any of the infectious disease stuff. But his Hippocratic oath had him firmly by the short and curlies. He had to stay here and help look after these people. He had to work with the team from the DPA. He had a responsibility. To them. To the patients. To the staff. To Callie…

Everything came back to her. No matter where his head drifted off to, she was always the thing he came back to. Like an anchor point.

He could almost see the picture of Helen that still sat on his desk at home. Her smiling face, dark hair and dark eyes. Home? When was the last time he'd gone home? When was the last time it had felt like home?

He sagged against the wall again. Everything was bubbling to the surface, thanks to the way he was feeling towards Callie, and he just couldn't deal with this—not on top of the DPA issue all over again.

Did she even realize how hard this was for him? To be amongst these people again? To be amongst the people that reminded him at every glance of how much he'd failed his wife?

What kind of a husband couldn't save his wife? Maybe for a regular guy that could be acceptable. But he was a doctor. And his wife had died from a medical complaint. One that, under normal circumstances, could have been treated and her life saved.

For a few hours with Helen he'd felt as if they had been trapped on a runaway train.

They hadn't got to experience the joy of a positive pregnancy test. They hadn't got to celebrate their child's arrival, planned or not. He felt cheated out of so many experiences—all because they'd been in the wrong place at the wrong time.

Worst of all, he didn't know who to be angry at most. Himself? The DPA? Evan Hunter? Helen?

It had been Evan who had sent Helen into the field, not him. Even though she hadn't been feeling one hundred percent. None of them had had any suspicion she might be pregnant—not even Helen. But their baby had decided to defy the odds of their contraceptive of choice. And by the time they'd known, it had been too late.

A ruptured ectopic pregnancy in the middle of nowhere. There had only been one possible outcome.

He had to get past this. He had to move on. Everything about this situation was wrong.

He couldn't begin to work out his feelings towards his past and the guilt he felt, in this new situation and his pull towards Callie. He felt pressured. Callie was pressured. It wasn't the right time or the right place. He had to step back. He had to step away.

And from the hurt look in Callie's eyes, he'd already done that. Whether he'd planned to or not.

He could hear mumbled voices through the door. They sent a cool breeze dancing over his skin, covering his chest and arms in goose-bumps. He grabbed his scrub top and pulled it over his head.

He had to go out there. He had to act as if nothing had happened. He had to try and help Callie save face, because if word of this ever got back to Evan Hunter...

He had no intention of being around to face the fall-out.

He glanced at his watch. Forty-eight hours. That was how long he'd lasted when a beautiful woman had been dangled under his nose.

The pull was just too strong.

But everything about this was wrong. They would be together for the next fourteen days. Fourteen days and nights with Callie Turner.

And he'd just made it all worse.

His hand hesitated on the door handle.

Because now he knew how her skin felt. Now he knew how she reacted to his touch. Before he could only have imagined. And that could have kept him safe. That could have kept him on a reasonably even keel.

But now...

He closed his eyes. And it was Helen's face he saw. Helen's eyes. Helen's smile. The instant image made him jump.

The sear in his chest was instant. Like his heart was being twisted inside his ribcage. He couldn't do this. He couldn't do any of this.

Callie was a career girl. He used to be the same.

But now he was a getting-by kind of guy. In two weeks' time, for the second time in his career, he would walk away from the constraints of the DPA. And nothing would give him greater pleasure.

No. He could do this. He could keep his head down. He could stay out of her way. He could work the opposite shift from her. He could make sure they were never alone together. He could make sure that opportunity didn't knock again.

Because that would keep him safe.

Because he wasn't entirely sure how he would react.

He straightened his shoulders and walked out into the corridor.

It was empty. Callie and Dan were gone.

CHAPTER NINE

EVAN WAS IMPATIENT. The computer graphics filled the wide screen on the wall, mapping the potential spread across the world, along with the corresponding time-scale. It was hours and hours of hard work and dedication. Every eye in the place was fixed on the simulation. The color-coded icons were blinking at him, the red ones demanding his full attention.

He turned round and folded his arms across his chest. Violet was wearing red today too. Almost as if she was marking a claim on the piece of work she'd just created. A fitted, knee-length red dress with a black belt capturing her waist. It was an unusual color for her to wear and he was surprised by how much it suited her. Her blonde hair sat on her shoulders and she peered through matching red-rimmed glasses. It was almost as if she was trying to divert his attention...

Then it struck him—she was.

His mind drifted back to a few months ago and a blurry night with drinks after work. She'd been wearing red then too. And he'd definitely been distracted. He felt the fire burn in his belly that she might have been thinking about that while getting dressed that morning and had deliberately chosen her outfit accordingly. His own thoughts made him feel distinctly uncomfortable and, consequently, irritable.

"Where's the stuff on Sawyer?" he snapped.

"What?" Delicate lines creased her forehead. She looked at him as if he was talking a foreign language.

"You know what," he accused. This was all becoming more and more obvious. "I asked you to do a background check on Sawyer. Find out where he's been and what he's been doing. I asked you more than two days ago. Where is it?"

She waved her hand in at him irritation. "Earth to Evan. I've been kind of busy on the save-the-planet-from-smallpox stuff."

He pulled his shoulders back in shock. Cheeky. Insolent. Not the way that Violet Connelly ever spoke to anyone—least of all him, her boss. She was really pushing him. And it didn't help that every time she came into his field of vision his eyes fixed on her lips.

Lips of which he'd already had experience.

He could see some ears pricking up around them, People craning their necks above their partitions to see how he was going to react.

Did anyone here know what had happened between them?

He had to make sure there were no suspicions. He couldn't let anyone think he would give Violet preferential treatment.

He placed a hand on her desk and leaned forward, drawing his head level with hers. Up close and personal she was a tiny little thing. His hands could probably span her waist. He could see her nibbling her bottom lip as if she was nervous. And she probably was with his big frame towering over her.

He pulled back a little and kept his voice calm. It

wasn't his job to entertain the crowds—they had enough work to be getting on with. "Dr. Connelly, I gave you a specific task to do a number of days ago. I expect you to have completed it." He caught the glimmer in her eye. It definitely wasn't fear. It was much more like rebellion!

"I've been busy." The words were firm, even if he could see the slight tremble in her hand as she picked up a pen.

"You're telling me that in the last two days you've found out nothing about Matt Sawyer? Nothing?" His voice was steadily rising now, despite his best intentions.

Was he imagining it or had she just pouted her lips at him? This woman was going to drive him crazy.

She shrugged her shoulders. "Oh, I've looked. But there's nothing to find. I've no idea what Matt Sawyer's been doing or where he's been." She raised one eyebrow at him and tilted her chin. "Why don't you ask him?"

She was baiting him. In front of a room full of colleagues. The hairs were standing on end at the back of his neck. It was all he could do not to growl at her.

"You've got two hours, Violet. Two hours to find out exactly what I requested on Matt Sawyer. If you don't deliver, I'm taking it to the director."

He turned on his heel and walked out of the room. The pen still dangling from Violet's fingers.

"Still nothing?"

The DPA guy shook his head as Sawyer leaned against the wall. It had been three days and they still had no word on the classification of the disease. They were still stuck in the no-man's land of a "brick-shaped orthopox", which told them something but pretty much told them nothing at the same time.

Sawyer had been doing his best impression of the invisible man. And it made him feel lousy.

When Callie worked days, he worked nights. When Callie was in the apartment, he was out, finding any excuse to be somewhere else. There had been a few awkward moments, a few "almost" bumps in the corridor, resulting in both of them jumping and staring at walls and floors instead of the person right before their eyes. A huge amount of avoidance tactics on his part.

He was beginning to find it almost comedic. The number of times he'd heard her voice behind a door he had been about to open, only to swerve and end up in a place he really didn't want to be, having conversations with people he barely knew.

On the other hand, yesterday he'd found himself in the children's playroom, leading the Portuguese soccer team on a quest for worldwide domination against the children in the US soccer team. It had been game controllers at dawn. But he'd had to let them win, even though he'd suspected they were playing dirty.

There were five kids, aside from Ben and Jack, in the containment facility, of varying ages and nationalities. None seem to have had any side-effects from the vaccine. And the minor ailments that had brought them into the E.R. in the first place had all been resolved. It was amazing what the threat of an infectious disease could do.

But spending time with the children had been fun. They were treating everything like a vacation. They could watch want they wanted on cable, play a mountain of console games and pretty much eat whatever they liked. He'd made a mental note that the children's playroom was now going to be his number-one place to go to avoid Callie.

Today had been torture. The trouble with a containment facility was that no matter how hard you tried to find somewhere else to sleep there really wasn't anywhere else to go so he had to stick to the apartment he'd been allocated.

The aroma of coffee had drifted under his door around lunchtime. He was supposed to be sleeping, but he'd only dozed on and off for a few hours. The temptation to get out of bed with his nose leading him directly to the coffee pot had been huge, but then he'd heard her voice. Callie was obviously in the kitchen, grabbing a bite to eat. And the last thing he wanted to do in his sleep-deprived state was run into her.

She was already destroying the few hours' sleep he was actually getting by invading his dreams. Sometimes happy, sometimes angry, but always in state of undress. Funny, that. It was taking him back to his teenage years.

And that probably wasn't a place he wanted to go. Violet had enough blackmail material on his misspent youth to last a lifetime.

The trouble with avoiding Callie was being out of the loop of information. She was the focal point around here—all paths led to Callie and if he wasn't communicating with her, he didn't always know exactly what was going on.

He had been sure that the DPA would have had a more definitive diagnosis by now. Frank Palmer would be working flat out. It didn't matter that he knew it could take up to seven days. He wanted to know *now*.

One of the nurses came and touched his shoulder. "Can you take a look at Mrs. Keating, Ben and Jack's mum? She's not feeling too good."

His stomach plummeted. It was the one thing they had all been waiting for—someone else to show signs of infection. He picked up Jill Keating's notes and started walking across the corridor. The thick bundle was packed full of assessments and observation notes. For a woman with no significant disease history it was surprising how quickly notes filled up in an isolation facility.

"What's she complaining of?" he asked the nurse.

There was another person that was having trouble looking at him.

But for an entirely different reason. The nurse's eyes would be full of unspoken worries and unanswered questions. Things that nobody wanted to say out loud right now.

Everyone was dreading someone showing signs of infection. It would give them all the confirmation of the infectious disease without the laboratory diagnosis.

"She has a low-grade temperature and a headache. Her pulse is fine and her blood pressure only slightly raised. But she's vomited twice."

Mrs. Keating was lying in bed in the darkened room. It had taken her more than forty-eight hours to finally leave the room that her children were in and have some rest. The woman was probably exhausted and that could explain the headache and the slight rise in blood pressure. But the temperature and vomiting?

He pulled on the protective clothing, regulation mask and gloves and pushed open the door. "Hi, Jill. It's Dr. Sawyer. Want to tell me how you're doing?"

She averted her eyes straight away as the light from the corridor spilled into the room. It sent an instant chill down his spine. "Wake Callie," he whispered over his shoulder to the nurse.

He spent the next twenty minutes examining Jill. She was definitely exhausted. And despite being surrounded by food and drink she was showing clinical signs of dehydration. The black circles under her eyes were huge and she vomited into a sick bowl again during his examination.

Callie was standing at the window in the corridor, looking anxiously through the glass. He'd signaled to her to wait outside.

She moved to the door as he came back outside and waited impatiently while he discarded his protective clothing.

"Well? What do you think?"

He started scribbling some notes on Jill's prescription chart. "I'm sorry that I woke you, Callie."

"Why? Is she okay?"

He nodded. "I can't say for certain but I suspect she is in the throes of her first-ever migraine. The only thing that doesn't really fit is the low-grade pyrexia. But everything else makes me think it's a migraine. And after the stress she's been under I wouldn't be surprised. I'm going to give her an injection then sit here and wait until her symptoms subside."

"And will they?"

He shrugged his shoulders. "I certainly hope so. This is a wait-and-see option. We need to give it a little time. An hour or so."

"Call me if there's any change."

He nodded. Disappointed. He'd half expected her to wait with him. This could be crucial in determining the nature of this disease. But it obviously wasn't to be. She couldn't get away from him fast enough.

And he couldn't really blame her.

Or maybe she was just showing faith in his competence as a doctor?

Whatever it was, he was just going to have to get

over it. But his stomach was gnawing at the memory of how much he'd missed those eyes in the last few days.

His nose picked up the smell of toasted bagels. It was time to follow his stomach. This could be a long wait.

An hour later Jill was in a deep sleep. The migraine relief seemed to have worked well and Sawyer was breathing a sigh of relief. He'd checked on the boys—both Jack and Ben were stable and showing no obvious signs of improvement or deterioration. It was four a.m. That horrible point of the night when nausea abounded and sleep seemed so far away.

He looked around. One of the nurses touched his shoulder. "Go and have some coffee, Sawyer, you look like crap."

"Thanks for that."

She smiled at him. "Oh, you're welcome. I'll page you if I need you—but I doubt it."

He headed down the darkened corridor. There was definitely a pot of coffee on the go somewhere. The smell seemed to be drifting towards him and making him follow it like the children had followed the pied piper. And he could hear some background noise.

He reached one of larger communal kitchens. The coffee pot was just on the boil. Just the way he liked it. Straight, black and hot.

He poured a cup and headed towards the noise. The kids must have left the TV on in the cinema room. It was something sappy. He slumped into one of the seats. If he just sat down for five minutes and drank this coffee, he would be fine. The caffeine would hit his system and keep him awake for the last few hours.

Five minutes.

"What are you doing here?"

He jumped. The voice cut through the darkness and he spilled hot coffee all down the front of his scrub trousers. "Hey!" He rubbed frantically at the stain, lifting the wet trousers from his groin area—some things just shouldn't get burned.

Callie appeared at his side and peered at the spreading stain. "You klutz." She started to snigger. That crazy middle-of-the-night kind of laugh that night shift staff got and couldn't stop.

Sawyer sighed and set down his half-filled coffee cup. "I came down here for a coffee to help me stay awake and wondered what the noise was. What are you doing here?"

"I couldn't get back to sleep."

"So you came down here, rather than sit up with me next to the patients?" It sounded almost accusing and he didn't mean it to come out that way but in the middle of the night social niceties disappeared.

"I guess I didn't want to sit next to you, Sawyer."

Yip. It worked both ways. Night shift certainly did away with the social niceties.

He didn't want to get into this. Not here. Not now. He glanced at the big screen. "You told me you were an action girl, not a chick-flick girl. What happened?"

Their eyes turned in unison at the screen as the hero's eyes followed the heroine, staring at her unashamedly.

Even in the dark Callie's cheeks looked a little flushed. Maybe it was the intimacy of the scene. Not intimate in that sense. But intimate in the fact it was the first time the audience could see how smitten the hero was with the girl of his dreams.

And he could relate.

Here, in the middle of a darkened room, in the midst of an outbreak, Sawyer could totally relate.

He could see Callie's long eyelashes, the blue of her eyes dimmed by the light. But the flickering screen highlighted her cheekbones, showing the beautiful structure and lines of her face. He couldn't take his eyes off her.

Her eyes met his. "I am an action girl. But I was too late this time. It seems the kids are action fans too—and they all have DVD players in their rooms." Her voice was quiet, almost whispered. It made him naturally lean towards her to hear what she was saying above the background noise of the movie.

"I'm an action girl" were the words playing around in his mind.

She held up another DVD and tilted her head to the side, revealing the long line of her neck.

His hand went automatically to her waist and she didn't flinch, didn't move. Her arm stayed half in the air, still holding up the DVD, almost as if she was frozen.

Sawyer stepped forward, the full length of his body next to hers. He forgot about the damp coffee stain on his scrubs. This was where he should apologize. This was where he should tell her he was having trouble getting his head around all this.

This was where he should tell her about Helen. About the fight with Evan and the consequences. This was where he should clear the air.

Because if he didn't, he'd never move on.

But he didn't do any of those things.

He just kissed her.

His hands captured her head, winding his fingers through her hair and anchoring her in position.

But he didn't kiss her like he had before.

This time he was gentle. This time he was slow. This

time he wanted her to know that he meant it. It wasn't just a reaction. It wasn't just a physical thing.

This was him, Matt Sawyer, wanting to make a connection with her, Callie Turner.

So he started on her lips. Brushing his against hers then moving along her jaw and down her neck.

He was just working his way back up the other side of her neck when Callie's hands connected with his shoulders, pushing him back firmly.

"No, Sawyer. Stop it."

He was stunned and immediately stepped away.

Even in the dark he could see tears on her cheeks. "I can't do this. This isn't me. And I know you don't mean it. I can't do what we did a few days ago and then just walk away. You need to leave me alone." She started walking towards the door. Away from him. "Just leave me, Sawyer. Leave me alone."

"Callie, wait—" But his words were lost because she'd almost bolted out the door. He stared down at his hands. The hands that had just touched her. That hands that still wanted to be touching her.

He didn't blame her. His earlier actions had been pretty much unforgiveable. But the pull towards her was real. And it wasn't going to go away any time soon.

He sagged back down into one of the chairs. There was no point in going after her right now.

He needed the proper time and space to talk to her.

His eyes went back to the screen flickering in the darkness. They'd reached the point in the movie where the heroine was telling the hero she was marrying someone else.

Kind of ironic really.

Callie flew along the corridor as if she were being chased by swarm of angry bees. He'd kissed her again. And she'd been so close to responding to him. So close.

But she couldn't let that happen again. She couldn't be caught in a compromising position with Sawyer. She had to keep her mind on the job.

That was the rational part of her brain talking.

Her heart was saying something else entirely.

She couldn't let him touch her again. She couldn't let him evoke those feelings in her again, only to walk away without a single glance.

She wasn't built that way. She couldn't deal with things like that.

Isabel had been entirely different. *Isabel* would have been the one kissing Sawyer and walking away without a second thought. She had always been in control.

Not like *her*.

History had taught her that she hated things she couldn't control. And there were lots of elements of this spinning out of her control, without adding her feelings for Sawyer into the mix.

When were these feelings ever going to go away? She'd thought working at the DPA where she and Isabel had planned to be would have given her some comfort. But in the end it hadn't.

The guilt she felt about her sister still gnawed away at her. She constantly compared herself to Isabel, without ever really meaning to.

Even with the men she'd dated she'd kept her sister at the forefront of her mind. Would Isabel have approved? Would she have liked this one? Would she have thought that one good enough?

But with Sawyer it was different. She didn't even want to give them space together in the same thought. Why was that?

If Sawyer had met Isabel, would he have been attracted to her instead of Callie?

That thought made her feel physically sick. She felt a horrible creeping sensation over her skin, along with a realization of her continued exasperation with herself.

When would this go away? When would she feel as if she was living her own life and not doing penance for the loss of her sister's?

Everything in her work and personal life was so mixed up right now. And being stuck in an enclosed space with Sawyer wasn't helping.

Yesterday she'd spent time fretting over the plan. While all her instincts had told her that keeping the brothers together was ultimately the right decision, the truth was that the plan told her otherwise.

She'd spent a few hours weighing up the pros and cons of insisting the plan be followed before finally deciding to let it go. The only thing was, unease still gripped her. Gnawed away at her stomach and kept her awake at night.

Plans were evidence based. Plans had been re-searched within an inch of their lives. How would she defend her decision if challenged from above?

Sawyer had whispered to her to relax and stop fol-lowing the plans a few nights ago and the truth was it hadn't been nearly as scary as she'd thought.

Just like making the decision about the brothers.

Her phone buzzed in her pocket and she pressed the answer button straight away. It was five in the morning so it had to be the DPA.

"Callie? How are you? How are you holding up?" Her footsteps froze.

"Callum?"

"Who else would call you at this time in the morn-ing?"

Relief flooded through her and the tears that had just vanished came spilling down her cheeks again.

Callum. Her port in a storm. The one person she actually *did* want to talk to.

"You don't know how happy I am to hear your voice. How are you, Callum?"

She heard the hearty laugh she was so used to. The familiar sound made her miss him all the more.

"I'm fine. You were right—it was an MI. They whipped me down to the angio lab and inserted a stent. Missed most of the last few days because of the drugs. But I'm feeling great today."

She leaned against the wall, sliding down onto her haunches. "If you're feeling great, why are you phoning me at five in the morning? Shouldn't you be resting?"

"Resting's for amateurs. Couldn't sleep and no one at the DPA will tell me anything useful. I blackmailed one of the nurses into letting me use her phone. It's been five days and I should have been officially discharged by now. Funny thing is, my doc won't discharge me to the containment unit."

She shook her head at his tenacity. She wouldn't put it above Callum to try and discharge himself straight to the containment unit. "You phoned the DPA?"

"Of course I did. I wanted to know how my favorite doctor was getting on."

She felt warmth spread across her chest. "I bet you say that to all the girls." It was so good to hear his voice. She'd heard about the stent but no one would actually say if they'd spoken to him. This made all the difference. She smiled. "And anyway who is your favorite doctor—me or Sawyer?"

He paused. Obviously deciding what to say next. "Yeah, Sawyer. Well, he used to be my favorite but you've taken over from him now. How are you getting on with him, Callie?"

His voice sounded a little strained. And the realization hit her. That's why he was phoning. That's why he was trying to get to the containment unit. He was worried.

"Ask me something else."

"Oh, I see. It's like that."

That was Callum. He knew her too well. She couldn't lie to him and try and dress this up but she didn't want to add to his stress. "Yes, it is. Ask me about the smallpox."

She heard the sigh at the end of the phone. "I'm assuming you don't have a definitive diagnosis yet."

"You're assuming right. We know it's an orthopox and we know it's definitely not chicken pox. We've vaccinated all those exposed and moved to the containment facility. What was this place, by the way? I'm assuming you know."

He cleared his throat. "It's just a little place that was on the back burner."

"What does that mean? The building is old, but the facilities are state-of-the-art." Her curiosity was piqued now—no matter what the time.

"How are the patients?"

She gave half a smile. An obvious deflection. He knew it. And she knew it. Whatever this building had been, he'd no intention of telling her. "We've got two sick little boys—one ventilated. And we're monitoring symptoms in everyone else. Had a bit of a scare with the boy's mother but it turned out to be nothing. Oh, that reminds me. We had someone we couldn't vaccinate. A nurse who is eighteen weeks pregnant. She's currently holed up for a fortnight in an exclusive Chicago hotel."

"Oh, no." Callum's silence was ominous. She'd expected him to say something else or to ask more questions.

"Callum?"

"How's Sawyer? Was he okay about that? How did he deal with the pregnant nurse?"

She shifted her weight from one leg to the other. What could she say? That initially he had freaked out? But he'd managed to contain how he'd been feeling and had done the job? It was truthful, but was probably too near to the bone. "He was fine. I know that his pregnant wife died on a DPA mission but no one really knows the details. Want to fill me in?"

His answer was brusque. "Not really. Is he following protocol?"

"Ours or his?"

"So it's like that. I might have guessed. Sawyer's never going to change." Even though he sounded a little exasperated, Callie could almost see the smile on his face as he said the words.

"If you tell me about him, Callum, maybe I'll understand him a little better. Maybe it will help us work together."

She could almost hear his brain ticking over at the end of the phone. "Are you having major problems with him? Professional problems?"

How did she answer that question? Because, like it or not, the professional problems were minor. It was the personal problems that were the real issue.

Callum had never been slow off the mark. He was a man who could always read between the lines.

"It sounds as if it's not up to me to tell you, Callie. It would be better coming from him." Words of wisdom from a man who was obviously seeing things much more clearly than she was. "Maybe I should give Sawyer a ring. Have you got his number? Did he ever change it?"

"Maybe you should relax. Maybe you should follow the post-MI protocol like a good patient."

"Give me his number."

"No."

"Dr. Turner, I asked for his number." His voice was rising now and he was obviously getting agitated. He only ever called her Dr. Turner when he was trying to tell her off. It made her smile.

"I'm hanging up now, Callum."

"Don't you dare!"

"Take care now."

She was smiling but still close to the floor on her haunches. Her legs were beginning to cramp.

She stood up and arched her back, trying to release the tension. Her head was beginning to thump, probably from lack of sleep and all the stress she was under. Nothing to do with Sawyer.

Nothing at all…

Sawyer was lying on his bed, trying to get some sleep. He glanced at his watch for the tenth time. The sun was streaming through the windows. Seemed like no one had thought of blackout blinds for this place.

He picked up his phone and pressed in Violet's number. His guilt was starting to kick in now. He should have phoned her earlier. His excuses were weak—even he knew that.

She picked up straight away and let out a big sigh. "Perfect timing, bruv."

He sat up in bed. The chance of sleep was long gone. "What's up?"

He heard her slow intake of breath. "I've got Evan Hunter breathing down my neck. He wanted me to check up on you—find out what you've been doing these last few years."

"Well, I'll make it easy for you. I don't want you to be next on Evan Hunter's hit list. Check out Borneo, Alaska and Connecticut."

"What?" He could almost hear the wheels spinning in her brain at the eclectic mix of places he'd been in the last six years.

"There's nothing sinister to find, Violet. You know that."

Her answer was instant. "I know that, Matt."

"What's Evan's problem? No—scratch that. I know what his problem is—me. But what exactly does he think he's going to find?"

Violet sounded annoyed. "I have no idea. He threatened to report me to the director if I didn't get back to him with a report in two hours."

"What? He asked you do to a report in the middle of the night?"

"Well, not exactly. He first asked me to do it five days ago. Then he gave me the two-hour time limit three days ago."

"And you still haven't done it?"

He could hear the casualness in her voice. "Yeah, well, I didn't really think he'd complain about me to the director. He was just growling at me. Trying to show me who's boss. Now you've given me the heads up I'll at least go and give him that to chew over. It should be enough to finally satisfy him you're not involved in this." He could hear the hesitation in her voice. "How are you, Sawyer? Is everything okay? Any other symptoms?"

"Not yet. We had a little scare earlier but it's fine. I'm fine." He paused. "Well, actually, I'm not fine."

There was a long significant pause at the end of the phone and he knew why. He'd never discussed anything with his sister before. He avoided personal issues at all costs.

"What's wrong?" Her voice was quiet, almost afraid to ask the question.

"It's Callie."

"Is something wrong with Callie? Does she have symptoms?" It was only natural for her to jump to the most obvious conclusion.

"No. It's not that. I kissed her."

"You did what?"

Well, that had got her attention. Other than their last conversation, he couldn't remember the last time Violet had ever shouted at him. But, then again, she was also defying Evan Hunter left, right and center, which was also unheard of. It seemed his sister had turned into a whole new person over the last six years. All while he'd been hiding in the outer parts of the planet.

"I kissed her." He flopped back down on the bed. The words seemed so much worse now he'd finally said them.

But they felt so much better. It was nice to finally offload.

"Why on earth did you kiss Callie Turner?" her voice hissed down the phone. She was obviously trying to keep anyone from hearing.

Sawyer felt like a teenager. Why did any guy kiss a pretty girl? "Because I wanted to. And I think she wanted me to."

"You mean she didn't slap your face?"

"Not quite."

Violet was obviously a bit stunned. "So, what's the problem?" She hesitated a second. "I mean, this isn't the first time you've kissed someone since Helen, is it?"

He let out a snort of laughter. "I think I can safely say no to that. But this is different."

"Different how?"

She'd put him on the spot now and he didn't quite know how to answer. "Different because I don't want to hurt her. But there's a definite attraction between us. And I know she feels it too."

"Has an alien inhabited your body?"

"What do you mean?"

"I mean that for the first time in years you're talking to me about your feelings. Since when have you done that?"

He couldn't answer.

"Okay, brother, I'm only going to say one thing. I like Callie. I mean, I *really* like her."

"Well, I think I like her too." There. He'd admitted it. To someone other than himself.

"Then don't mess this up. Don't hurt her." The words were blunt and straight to the point. Violet had never been one to mess around with how she felt.

"Can't you give me something else? Can't you tell me to handle this? You know her better than I do." He was beginning to sound desperate, but right now he didn't care.

"Really? Well, here's the clincher—I haven't been in a lip-lock with her, Matt. And I'm sorry but you don't reach the grand old age of thirty-six and ask your sister for dating advice. That ship sailed a long time ago, buddy. Probably around the time you told everyone about my high-school crush."

He cringed but it brought a smile to his face. He'd

made a poster and stuck it up outside the school. Violet had locked herself in her room and hadn't spoken to him for days. She still hadn't got over it.

"So, no advice, then?"

"Absolutely not. Not on your love life anyway. Just stay safe, brother. And phone me if there's any problem. Any *work*-related problem."

"What about Evan?"

Her voice had a hard edge to it now. "Leave me to worry about him. I'm hoping I'll be out of his hair soon enough." She hung up before Sawyer had a chance to ask her what she meant.

He stared at the ceiling. Potential smallpox day five. Great.

CHAPTER TEN

"WAKE UP, SAWYER."

One of the nurses stood above him. Liz? Julie? He really couldn't remember. He sat bolt upright in the bed, not even thinking about hiding himself.

She turned sideways. "Cover yourself up, boy. And get dressed. Some guy from the DPA wants to talk to either you or Callie, and I can't find her."

Sawyer pulled the sheet half across his body, lifting a crumpled pair of scrubs from the floor and tugging them on. He smirked as the nurse rolled her eyes and handed him the matching top.

He let out a laugh as she walked to the door then stopped and threw him a can of deodorant. Then something registered with him. "What do you mean, you can't find Callie? Where can she be?"

The nurse shrugged. "I just know the guy said he had to speak to either one of you. He's been holding for a few minutes because I tried to find Callie first. When I couldn't, he said to wake you."

"Where's the phone?"

"At the nurses' station."

He jogged along the corridor. His brain was in overdrive. It was day seven. This had to be a diagnosis. But where on earth was Callie?

He picked up the phone. "Frank?"

"Finally. Sleeping beauty wakes up."

"Have you got something?"

"Is this Frank? Is this the man who is supposed to be in Hawaii with his devoted and gorgeous wife, who'd bought eight different bikinis for our long-awaited vacation?"

Seven days. He'd waited seven days for this. "Frank?" He couldn't hide the impatient tone in his voice.

"It's monkeypox."

"What?" Sawyer was stunned. He'd never seen monkeypox before. It had never really been on his radar.

Frank seemed to know exactly what to say. "You'll need to examine the boys again for bites, scratches and abrasions. Monkeypox usually only occurs in Western or Central Africa but strangely enough the last known case was in the U.S. in 2003, caused by prairie dogs."

"What?" Nothing about this made sense. His brain couldn't process what he was hearing.

"Monkeypox can be spread by squirrels, dogs, rats, mice and rabbits. That's why your boy had swollen glands. It's one of main differences in symptoms between smallpox and monkeypox."

Sawyer ran his hand through his hair. Where was Callie? He had to talk to her about this straight away. Things were starting to register in his brain. Should he have guessed this? He hadn't given too much thought to the swollen lymph glands—even though they were unusual in smallpox. He'd just assumed it was a viral response.

"What are our options?"

Frank cleared his throat. "None, really. No known treatment. It's less severe than smallpox and the smallpox vaccine can lessen the symptoms. But it can still be fatal—monkeypox can have a one to ten percent mortality rate. All the smallpox infection controls should remain in place."

They spoke for a few more minutes then Sawyer replaced the receiver. "Wow." He leaned against the wall.

His head was spinning. His eyes swept across the room. Everyone was going about their business quietly and efficiently. What effect would this news have on the people here?

In a way it was a relief to finally have a diagnosis but with no known treatment it still made things difficult. He racked his brain, trying to remember what he could about monkeypox. It wasn't much.

He only hoped there was a plan.

Had he just thought that? Him, Sawyer, wondering if there was a plan?

Callie was obviously rubbing off on him.

Callie—where was she?

He started walking along the corridor, stopping people on the way past. "Have you seen Callie? Do you know where Callie is?" Time after time his colleagues just shook their heads.

Finally, one of the contact tracers furrowed his brow. "I saw her go down there a little while ago." He pointed down one of the long corridors.

Sawyer strode along. He couldn't remember this part of the building on the plan. It was well away from the small labs and isolation ward. He reached a double door at the end of the corridor and pushed it open.

It took his breath away.

The tiny little room was extraordinary. A small stained-glass window was set into the facing wall, with the sun streaming through causing a kaleidoscope of colors across the white walls. It was like a magical light show.

Callie hadn't even heard him enter. She was sitting on one of the wooden pews near the altar at the front. There was no particular religion celebrated here. It was one of those non-denominational rooms that could be used by anyone.

A quiet place. For contemplation.

He walked along the carpeted aisle and sat down next to her. She jerked, conscious of no longer being alone, and opened her eyes. He slid along a little. She was sitting directly in the stream of coloured light. Her face and skin were lit up like a rainbow. It was dazzling. He'd never wanted to reach out and touch anyone more than he did right now.

Papers were scattered all around the floor at her feet.

"What do you want, Sawyer?" She sounded weary, exhausted. The relief that had instantly flooded him when he'd heard the diagnosis disappeared. All of a sudden he could hear the countdown in his head. Now they had a definitive diagnosis, it was another step closer to getting out of there.

It was a step closer to getting away from the dreaded DPA. It was also a step closer to getting away from Callie.

And he wasn't prepared for the way that made him feel.

"Sawyer?"

He was still looking at her pale skin bathed in myriad colors. It was taking his breath away. As were the feelings sweeping over him.

He took a breath. "We have a diagnosis. It's monkeypox."

"Monkeypox?" Her voice rose automatically then she looked around her, as if conscious she shouldn't shout in a place of worship. She fell to her knees on the paper-strewn floor where papers had been tossed in all directions.

He joined her. "Do you think there's something about monkeypox in here?"

She nodded. "There is. It isn't much, just some basic information and guidelines." Her head shot back up, "Who did you speak to?"

"Frank. And before you ask, he was positive. He said you could call him back. He'll stay at the lab until he gets a chance to speak to you."

"Here it is!" She pulled a few crumpled pieces of paper from the floor. Her eyes started racing across the text. She was mumbling under her breath, "Same transmission precautions, slightly shorter incubation period." Her eyes lit up. "I'm not entirely sure—I'll need to check—but I think this is good news for Alison. It seems to be a larger droplet infection. There's a good chance she won't have been infected."

He nodded. "Actually, it still has a seventeen-day incubation period. She'll need to wait a little longer before she can go home."

Callie nodded but the smile reached all the way up to her eyes. "It's something. I was dreading a small-pox diagnosis."

"Me too." He looked around him. "How did you find this place?"

She let out a little laugh. "Curiosity got the better of me. It wasn't marked on the plans and I wanted to find out what was down here." She put her hands out. "Once I'd found this place I wanted to keep this little piece of paradise to myself."

"I don't blame you." His eyes met hers. He didn't want to fight. He didn't want a confrontation. Both of them knew they needed to talk. But this just wasn't the right time or place.

She looked down at the mess she'd made on the floor. A bright red folder had been pushed under one of the pews. "I came here to escape. To get out of the rat race." She edged the folder with her foot. "I had a bit of a disagreement with the plan. It sort of ended up all over the place."

He folded his arms and gave her a lopsided grin. "Shock, horror. Callie Turner threw the plan away?"

"I guess I did." She was biting her lip as she stared at the scattered papers. Didn't she know how much that distracted him?

He rested back against the wooden pew. Not exactly designed for comfort. Any minute now Callie would be off, her brain kicking into gear and taking off at full speed. He could picture her talking nineteen to the dozen and shouting instructions to everyone.

That's why he kind of liked this place.

"How long have you had this hidden gem?"

She arched her eyebrow at him and had the good grace to look embarrassed. "A few days. Right after we bumped into each other in the kids' cinema room. I needed somewhere I could have a little space."

"From me?" He didn't want her to say yes. He *really* didn't want her to say yes. But somehow it was more important that she was honest with him than that his feelings were hurt.

She sighed. "From you, from me, from everything." She threw up her hands but her voice was remarkably steady. "I had to sort a few things out in my head." She gave him a sad sort of smile. "I spoke to Callum. He wanted to call you—to interfere—but I wouldn't let him."

It was probably the first time in his life that he didn't automatically jump to his own defense. He didn't need to. He knew exactly what she would have said to Callum and exactly what he would have said in response.

"So, is he going to kick my ass?"

She let out a little snigger.

"Just as well I changed my number, then." He turned to face her. "Seriously, is he well enough to call?"

She nodded.

"Do you mind if I call him and tell him about the monkeypox? It might be the only thing that distracts him from tearing me off a strip or two."

"I think that would be fine." She stood up, her feet brushing against her paperwork. She looked a little lost. "I'll come back for this later. I still haven't really figured out if this is the place for me. I need to do a little more thinking."

"The place for you?" He looked around him in confusion. "A chapel?"

She shook her head slowly and took a deep breath. "No. The DPA."

There it was, he thought. The thing that was bothering her most. Him kissing her had only been a distraction.

And it was obviously the first time she'd said it out loud.

The underlying issue was still there. She was uncomfortable. She wasn't truly happy in her work—he knew it and she knew it. He'd known it right from the beginning. So he wasn't the main cause of her problems, only an antagonist.

"You're doing a good job, Callie." It seemed important to tell her. It seemed important to rally her confidence.

"You think so?" She'd reached the door now and turned back to face him.

He nodded. "I do. And don't think about things too long, Callie. Take it from someone who knows. Sometimes while you're doing all that thinking, life passes you by."

She pulled her shoulders back as if she was a little startled by his words. Her hand wavered on the door-handle and then she came back and sat down beside him again.

It didn't matter that she had other things to do. Other news to spread. Other plans to follow. Sometimes you just had to act on instinct. To take the moment before it passed.

"Is that what happened to you, Sawyer? Life has just passed you by?"

He froze, lowering his eyes and taking a few breaths. Her hand crept over and held his, interlocking their fingers.

He nodded, still looking at the floor. "I've lost six years," he whispered "being angry at everyone and everything."

His gaze rose again and fixed on the wall in front of him, staring at the beautiful light streaming through the stained-glass window. She squeezed his hand. Sometimes it was better to say nothing. Sometimes it was better just to give someone the time to say what they needed. Sometimes the best gift to give to someone was just to listen.

It struck her like gold. This was part of what she wanted to do. Not just for Sawyer but for her patients too.

"I was angry with Evan for sending her into the field. I was angry with myself for not knowing my wife was pregnant. I was angry with Helen for not realizing she was pregnant."

He turned to face her. His eyes were wet with tears and he wrinkled his brow. "I was angry that the plan didn't have any contingencies for things like this—a member of staff needing surgical intervention in the middle of nowhere."

He took a deep breath. "But most of all I was angry at myself for not being able to save her. I was her husband. I should have been able to save her…"

She let his voice tail off. She wanted to put her arms around him. She wanted to hug him as tightly as she could.

But there was a balance here that could so easily be tipped. He'd shared something with her that she doubted he'd shared before. What did that mean?

It seemed almost like a step towards her. But she couldn't be sure. And was she ready to take a step like that while she still had demons of her own?

Something twisted inside her. Could she talk about Isabel? Was she ready to share? She was still faltering. She still had to step out of Isabel's shadow before she could do anything else. Too much was happening all at once, so where did Sawyer fit into this equation?

She rubbed her hand over the top of his. Words seemed so futile now but she had to say something so she kept it simple. "Thank you for sharing, Sawyer. I know it was hard. And I'm glad you did." Her words were whispered and he gave her a little smile.

"I think it's time you went outside and faced the masses. Better share the good news and tell them what they need to know."

She nodded and slowly stood up. He needed some time. He needed some space. She could appreciate that.

And if she really cared about him, she had to give it.

"Come out when you're ready." She gave him a little nod and walked out.

Sawyer leaned back against the pew. In a matter of minutes it would be chaos out there again. Everyone would have questions and be looking for answers. The people currently quarantined would need up-to-date information. They would need to know what would happen next. Everything would have to be reassessed, re-evaluated, reconfigured.

As soon as the door closed behind her, Sawyer felt the air in the room become still. He didn't feel any urge to hurry after her. It would all still be out there in a few minutes—or a few hours. It was truly peaceful in here. No outside noises and far enough away from the clinical areas and staff to shield it from any external influences. Not even the noise of the birds tweeting outside.

He sat there for the longest time watching the colorful reflections from the stained-glass window dance on the wall to his right.

He looked at the scattered pieces of the plan around his feet.

Plans. He'd spent so long hating plans and everything about them. Blaming them and the DPA for the part they'd played in Helen's death.

It didn't matter that he was supposedly an intelligent, rational man. Nothing about his wife's death had seemed rational to him.

It had all seemed so random.

The DPA planned for every eventuality—or so he'd thought. But it hadn't planned for that. It hadn't planned for his wife to collapse with an ectopic pregnancy in the middle of nowhere and too far away for any emergency treatment.

And it had made him mad.

It had made him behave in a way that would have embarrassed Helen. He had questioned everything. He had torn up plans and set them on fire. He'd refused to follow any of the protocols that the DPA had set. And then he'd walked away from it all.

He'd walked away because he hadn't wanted to deal with anything.

He couldn't possibly believe that they'd just been unlucky. That Helen's death had simply come down to dumb, rotten luck.

He'd tried to forget everything and push everyone away.

But now it was time to stop all that. It was time to open his eyes.

It was time to remember—both the good and the bad.

And he remembered. He remembered everything about his wife that he'd loved.

And for the first time in a long time he took joy in remembering.

The dark shade of her hair, the chocolate color of her eyes. The fact that every item in her wardrobe had been a variation of a shade of blue. Her collection of bells that had sat on the window ledge in their bedroom. The smell of her favorite perfume, which she'd worn every single day. The candles she'd lit around her bath at night. The grey and blue felt hat she'd worn in winter that he'd always said made her look one hundred and five.

All the things that he'd been terrified to forget. Once—just once—he'd forgotten who her favorite author had been. It had sent an irrational, horrible fear through his entire body. How could he forget something about his darling Helen? Those books were still sitting on her bedside cabinet.

So he'd made lists and chanted things over and over in his bed at night. He hadn't been able to stand the thought of her fading from his memory. That the love that he'd felt for her would ever die.

He remembered their first date at the movies, their first kiss, their first fight and their first home. Their wedding day. Their wedding night.

And the way he'd held her on that last, horrible day when they'd both known she was going to die.

That nothing could save her. Even though he kept telling her she'd be fine.

The way she'd felt in his arms as he'd felt the life slowly drain from her body.

The way she'd told him she'd love him forever. And to live a good life.

Here, in this special place, it felt right. It felt right to remember her. It felt like a celebration.

Of life.

Of love.

Of forgiveness.

A single tear rolled down his cheek. He'd cried an ocean's worth of tears but now it was time for the last one.

Now it was time to let go.

Now it was time to live his life.

CHAPTER ELEVEN

THE ALARM STARTED sounding sharply. Sawyer and Dan were on their feet almost simultaneously. Even though the ventilator was breathing for Jack, his blood results had shown that his organs were starting to fail.

"Cardiac arrest. He's in V-fib."

Sawyer was almost through the door before one of the nurses blocked his path. "Gown!" she shouted.

Dan hadn't been so forgetful and already had a gown half on and his mask in place. Sawyer hated this. What was the point? How effective were the masks really? How much protection did the gown really offer? Wouldn't it make more sense just to get in and defibrillate him?

He hauled the gown and mask on and entered the room just as Dan placed the paddles on the boy's chest. "Clear!"

Jack's little body arched and all eyes fixed on the monitor.

Still VF.

Callie ran into the room, her gown barely covering her shoulders. "No!" she gasped, and ran to the other side of the room.

It was then Sawyer heard the high-pitched squeal. The squeal of a little boy watching people attempt to resuscitate his brother and not having a clue what was going on. He cursed and pulled the curtain between the beds. Why hadn't he realized? Why hadn't he even thought of that?

But Callie had. She had her arm around Ben's shoulders and was whispering to him through her mask. Her face was mainly hidden but he could still see her eyes. And there were tears in them.

Dan was moving quickly, seamlessly, shouting instructions to the surrounding staff. Jack's mother and father appeared at the window, horrified at what was happening to their son.

Jill Keating promptly dissolved into a fit of tears, her legs giving way beneath her.

They started CPR, a nurse with a knee on the bed using one hand on Jack's small chest. Regular, rhythmic beats. It was painful to watch.

The ventilator had been unhooked. Another doctor was bagging Jack down the tube already in place.

Drugs were pushed through Jack's IV. Anything to try and restart his heart.

"Everyone stop a second!" Dan shouted.

Callie's head shot up, a look of horror on her face. She moved from Ben's bed over to where Sawyer was standing. "You can't stop!" she shouted. "Don't you dare stop!"

A hand tapped Violet on the shoulder. "You've to go the boardroom."

Her head shot up. "What for? I'm in the middle of something right now. Can't it wait?"

Maisey shook her head. "I seriously doubt it."

Violet spun around in her chair. Maisey's voice didn't

sound too good. "What do you mean?" She had a horrible feeling in the pit of her stomach.

"I'm sorry, Violet."

Violet reached out and grabbed her sleeve as she tried to walk away. "What do you mean, you're sorry? Why have I to go the boardroom?"

Maisey couldn't look her in the eye. "It's the director. Along with Evan Hunter. I think Evan's complained about the deadline you didn't meet—the report he's been waiting four days for."

Violet's heart started to thud in her chest. "But that's what I'm working on." She held up the crumpled piece of paper.

Maisey shook her head. "I'm sorry, Violet. The director said he wanted to see you straight away."

Violet stood up, trying to ignore the tremor in her legs.

Rats. She'd known she was treading on thin ice when she hadn't had the report ready for Evan on time.

The truth was she had been hoping he would forget all about it now they had a final diagnosis of monkeypox. Sawyer should be the last thing on his mind right now.

She scrabbled around her desk for the report she'd been writing. Not only was it very late, she'd also left the details scarce. It would hardly placate the director.

Was he about to fire her?

Was she about to get fired because she'd tried to cover for her brother?

Her heart pounded as she crossed the department on her way to the boardroom. At this rate she would be sick all over the director's shoes.

The boardroom—where all official business was carried out.

One thing was sure—if she was going down, she was taking Evan Hunter with her. Let Evan see what the director thought about the boss cavorting with his staff.

All heads turned towards her. Callie's heart was racing, sweat lashing off her brow and running down her back.

Sawyer stepped into her line of vision, blocking the view of Jack and the rest of the staff. It took her a second to focus.

"Callie. Calm down."

Her skin was prickling. The scar on her leg itching like crazy. Her head flicking back between Ben's fearful face on the bed behind her and Sawyer's wide frame standing in front of her.

Everything seemed to be spiraling out of her control. She didn't feel in charge any more. "We can't stop. We can't. It's not been long enough." She was shaking her head. This wasn't even her area of expertise. What did she know about resuscitating a child? The last time she'd been involved in a pediatric resuscitation she'd been a first-year resident. It had made her realize that pediatrics wasn't for her.

"Callie." His hands were firmly on her shoulders now. "Step away from this. It's under control."

That's when she lost it even more. "You think this is under control? Under control? How? How is this under control? Is this part of the plan?"

She moved closer to Sawyer and hissed in his ear, "If Jack's about to die, you need to tell his family. You need to give them a chance to say goodbye." Her eyes drifted back to the bed behind her. "You need to give Ben a chance to say goodbye. He should get to hold his brother's hand."

She was feeling frantic. She couldn't let this happen.

It didn't matter that she wasn't a pediatrician. She was the doctor in charge of this outbreak so, at the end of the day, everyone should be doing what she told them.

Sawyer reached up and stroked her cheek. The action took her by surprise. It brought her instantly back to the here and now. "Callie, Dan's not stopping. He's only waiting for a few seconds to recheck the cardiac monitor—to see if Jack's heart rhythm has changed. Think, Callie. We always do this at arrests. Don't we?"

His voice was quiet, only loud enough for her to hear. Not that the rest of the staff were bothering. Most were still round Jack's bed, assisting with the arrest. Another nurse had appeared at Ben's side and was sitting with her arm around him, talking in his ear.

Ben.

He was terrified. He was crying. He was asking the nurse questions. Callie felt herself start to shake.

"We've got a rhythm!"

Both their heads turned towards the shout. Dan had just defibrillated Jack's little chest again and the monitor had given a little blip. Dan started shouting more instructions for different drugs. The room was a hive of activity. IV's were being hung and Mr. and Mrs. Keating had been gowned up and were being shown into the room.

Callie was trembling. She couldn't stop herself.

Then a warm hand slipped into hers and pulled her out of the room, walking her along the corridor and sitting her down in an easy chair. A cold drink was pressed into her hands and Sawyer sat in the chair opposite her.

He didn't say a word. He just sat.

The cold juice slid down her throat. The intense itch in her leg increased. She was clawing at her leg and couldn't stop. He bent over, his hand capturing hers and stopping her scratching. His head was underneath hers and he looked up at her. "Want to tell me what just happened in there?"

She felt her throat constrict. "I don't think I can."

He sat back in his chair. She could tell he was contemplating what to do next. What on earth must he be thinking of her?

His gaze was steady. It felt as if he was looking deep inside her. Somewhere she didn't want him to go. "It's time, Callie. Tell me about your scar."

She took a sharp breath. How did he know? *How did he know there was a connection?*

She laid her palm flat on her thigh. The desire to scratch was overwhelming. but she knew it was all psychological. No matter how hard she scratched, it wouldn't stop the itch. She'd just end up breaking her skin and drawing blood.

"I was in a car accident." She didn't know where the words had come from. It almost felt as if someone else had said them. But it was definitely her voice.

"How long ago?" It was a measured question. A prompt. It was almost as if he knew she just couldn't come out and tell him everything at once—it would be too painful.

"I was twenty-three."

"Were you badly injured?"

She took a deep breath. Although the scar was a permanent reminder, for the most part Callie had pushed all memories of her injuries aside.

Physical injuries could heal. Psychological injuries not so much.

"I had a fractured femur and tib and fib. Fractured ribs too."

"Wow. You must have had to take some time out of medical school."

"Only a few weeks. I became their first official online student. They recorded lectures for me and sent me notes. I did my assignments online for a couple of months."

It almost gave the game away and she could see the calculating expression on his face. Her professors had gone above and beyond their responsibilities and he had to be wondering why. Most medical schools would have told a seriously injured student to take time off, recuperate and come back the following year.

His gaze remained steady. It was obvious that he'd figured things out. "Who else was in the car, Callie?"

She was instantly on the defensive. "What makes you think someone else was in the car?"

"Who else was in the car, Callie?"

He'd just repeated the question. There was no fooling Sawyer.

Her throat was instantly dry again and her voice cracked. "My sister, Isabel."

He moved forward and took her hands again. "Isabel. What a beautiful name. Tell me about your sister, Callie." Again he was surprising her. He wasn't hitting her with a barrage of questions, he was just giving her an open invitation to talk.

"I can't," she whispered, as a single tear slid down her cheek. This was just too hard.

He reached up and caught it in his fingertips. "Yes, you can."

Everything had just changed color for Sawyer. He already knew her sister must be dead. The look on her face had said it all and the hairs currently standing on end at the back of his neck agreed.

He could see how much she was struggling. He could tell she wanted to run from the room like a frightened rabbit. She'd barely been able to get the words out.

A sister. Callie had a sister. Or she'd *had* a sister.

Now he understood her reaction when she'd heard about Violet. Now he understood why she'd been so angry with him. If she'd lost a sister and felt as if he'd abandoned his…well, her reaction was entirely normal.

"Isabel was a year older than me. She was at medical school too. She wanted to work at the DPA."

"Did you?" Things were starting to fall into place for him. This was behind the reaction in the chapel earlier. This was why she wasn't sure of herself.

She hesitated. "I…I didn't know what I wanted to do."

"Was Isabel injured in the car accident?"

Callie couldn't speak now. She just nodded. The tears were spilling down her face. Her hands were icy, almost as if she was in shock. He rubbed them gently, trying to encourage the blood flow and get some heat into them again.

It was obvious that Callie didn't talk about this to people. Violet hadn't heard a single thing about this—he suspected that no one at the DPA knew. Hadn't anyone ever asked her about her scar?

It was one of the first things he'd noticed about her.

It was time to ask the ultimate question. He had to give her a chance to let go. "Did she die?"

And that's when the sobs were let loose. Big, loud gasping sobs. The kind where you couldn't catch your breath before the next one took over your body.

He knew how that felt. He'd been there too.

He moved, sitting on the arm of the easy chair, wrapping his arm around her shoulders and letting her rest her head on his shoulder as she cried. It was the most natural thing to do.

Grief was all-consuming.

"There was a nurse and she knew Isabel was going to die. My parents hadn't got there yet. They were about to take me to Theatre but she wouldn't let them. She pulled me over to Isabel and put her hand in mine. It was the best and worst moment of my life. She knew how important it was. And I never even got to thank her. Everything just turned into a blur after that. My parents arrived and..."

"That's why you wanted the boys to hold hands. Now I get it," he murmured. It all made sense now. The look of terror on her face, her reactions. They were all the actions of someone who had walked in those shoes. Only someone who'd had that experience could truly know what it all meant and how important the smallest thing could be.

Her voice tailed off. She couldn't talk any more. He lifted a damp lock of her hair and dropped a kiss on her forehead. "I understand, Callie. I understand better than you could ever know."

"How can you?" she whispered. Her whole body was shaking. "We were fighting. I've never told anyone this but Isabel and I were fighting. A car came round the corner on the wrong side of the road and I didn't have time to react. I didn't have time to react because I was distracted. I was trying to stop Isabel from getting her own way yet again."

He could see the pain written across her face. And more than anything he wanted to take it away.

The feelings almost overwhelmed him. It had been

so long since he'd felt like this that he almost didn't recognize it. That intensity. That urge to protect.

The feelings of love.

Sawyer sucked in his breath. The pain spread across his chest. His heart thudded, his muscles tensed.

Every one of his senses was hyper-aware. He could hear her panting breaths, feel the dampness of her tears between his fingertips. He could smell the aroma of her raspberry shampoo and remember the taste of her on his lips.

And he could see her. All of her. Her bedraggled hair, damp around her forehead. The little lines etched around her clear blue eyes. The pink tinge of her cheeks. The dark red of her lips.

Her pink scrub top clung to her, outlining her firm breasts and the curve of her waist. The matching trousers hugged her hips and thighs. Her bright pink casual shoes cushioned her feet, with one dangling from her silver-starred toes.

All of this made up the picture of the woman that he loved.

The realization made him want to run. Made him want to escape for a few minutes to sort his head out and realign his senses.

But he couldn't leave. He could never leave her like this. His hand rubbed her back and he tried to keep his eyes off her silver-starred toes and the pictures they were conjuring up in his mind.

"All siblings fight, Callie. That's normal. That's what being a brother or sister is all about. You were just unlucky."

She shook her head. "But it didn't feel like that." She pressed a hand to her chest. "Isabel had always been really competitive. Medical school was just making her worse." Her eyes turned to meet his. "Of course, her fellow students would never have said that. They all embraced that kind of lifestyle. As if everything was a race, every mark a victory. But she carried it home with her. And it made being her sister tough." Her voice cracked and sobs racked her shoulders once again.

Sawyer pulled her close. She was consumed with guilt. That much was obvious. Not just because she'd been driving the car but because of how she'd been feeling towards her sister.

"Callie, I know. I understand. Violet was the good girl in the family. The one who always looked perfect in pictures. Sometimes I even hated her."

"You did?" Her eyes widened, her expression was one of surprise.

"Of course I did—she's my sister. Family's like that. You can't love or hate anyone more than your immediate family. No one else generates the same emotional energy. The same tug. Even in love." He gave her a smile.

"I walked away a few years ago. If I'd stayed near my family they would never have allowed me to live the way I have. The first thing Violet did when I phoned her was chew me out. Just wait till I see her. There won't be anything left for you."

"For me?" The tone in her voice changed. Her gaze fixed on his.

He bent his face to hers, taking in her trembling lips. Right now he didn't care about the monkeypox. He didn't care about the quarantine and vaccinations. And he certainly didn't care about the plans.

All he cared about was the woman in front of him.

It didn't matter how long he'd known her. It didn't matter how much they'd have to work through. All that mattered now was that he wanted a chance with her.

A chance to see where life could take them.

"Callie, what would it take to make you happy?"

She shook her head. "What do you mean?"

He knelt down in front of her. "I want you to stop thinking about anyone else. Stop thinking about the situation we're in with work. Stop thinking about responsibilities. Stop thinking about what anyone else thinks about you." He clasped both her hands in his. "I've spent the last six years in a fog, Callie, and being around you has finally woken me up."

He looked around the plain white room they were in. "I can see the color in things again. I can see light again. And it's all because of you."

She took a deep breath and drew back a little. She looked scared. Not of him—but of what he was saying.

"But we're not a good match, Sawyer. We're nothing alike. Even Callum said we're like oil and water."

Sawyer smiled. Trust Callum to see things long before anyone else could.

"And opposites attract, Callie." He drew her closer and whispered in her ear, "And in case you haven't noticed, I'm really attracted to you."

"Ditto," she whispered.

Their eyes met. They were reliving the conversation in the kids' cinema room.

"Callie, do you really want to be part of the DPA?"

"What?" She looked shocked.

He held his hands out. "This, Callie, all this. Is this really what you want? Because I can see you're a good doctor but I have to keep convincing you of that." He laid his palm on her chest above her heart, "And if you don't feel it in here, I wonder if you're doing the job of your heart or if you're just doing your duty to your sister."

All of a sudden she couldn't meet his all-too-perceptive gaze.

He put a finger under her chin and gently made her look at him. "Sometimes you need someone else to put things into perspective for you. Callie, I see a beautiful woman who is a great doctor but who is clearly in the wrong job. Was it in your heart to come to the DPA? Or did you come because that was the path that Isabel had mapped out for you both?"

"We wanted to work together. It was our dream."

"Both your dreams? Or only hers?"

"Don't say that. I don't like the way you make that sound. It was our plan." Her eyes drifted away from his and became fixed on the blank wall. "When you don't follow the plan, things go wrong. That's what happened that night. I took a different road—I was just so sick of Isabel being in charge all the time. Planning what we were doing every second of every day. Even down to what we ate."

Her shoulders started to shake again, her widened eyes turning back to meet his. "Don't you see what happened? When you stick to the plan, things go fine. But when you don't…that's when things go wrong. We would never have been on that road if I hadn't fought with Isabel. If I'd just gone along with what she'd wanted, everything would have been fine."

"You don't know that. You *can't* know that." He touched her cheek. "And would you have liked this job any more if Isabel was working next to you? Or would you still hate it just as much but do a better job at hiding it—all to keep her happy? To stick to the plan?"

She opened her mouth to speak but Sawyer wasn't finished. "Sticking to the plan doesn't always work. Helen and I stuck to the plan. The plan didn't cover what to do in a surgical emergency with no equipment in the middle of nowhere. Because that's all it was—a plan. Nothing more, nothing less. Just another tool to have in your box. Life has a funny way of making its own plan, no matter what's down in black and white."

"And if you don't like it?"

"That's the beauty of having a plan, Callie. Knowing when to use it and knowing when to drop it." He crouched down in front of her, "Thinking of Isabel, does it still hurt?"

She hesitated. "Yes." Her voice was barely audible.

"Callie, if Isabel were here right now, what would she say to you?"

Callie shifted in her seat. "She'd tell me to get my act together." She looked Sawyer in the eye, "She'd tell me not to get distracted by other people. She'd tell me not to waste the last nine years of my career by throwing away my role in the DPA now." Was she trying to convince him or her?

"And if she could see you now—if she could feel how you felt every day at work? Do you honestly think that's what she'd say?"

Callie sighed and he could see light dawn across her face. She was finally going to stop giving the answers she was expected to give. "No. She'd give me a boot up the ass and ask me why I hadn't said something sooner."

He smiled at her. "I think I would have liked Isabel."

She buried her head in her hands. "What will my parents think if I tell them I don't want to do this any more? They'll be so disappointed." Her voice drifted off and he could see pain flit across her eyes again.

"Callie, they've lost one daughter. They've gone through the worst pain imaginable. All they could want for you is to be happy."

He put his hand back on her heart. "Think of me as your own Aladdin's genie. I'm going to grant you a wish. And I'll do everything in my power to make it happen. What is it that you want, Callie?"

She was looking into his eyes, searching his face. He could tell she was terrified of revealing what she really wanted. He prayed he wasn't making her take a step too far.

But this felt right. It wasn't just him who needed to move on—it was her too. And they could do it together. Because nothing else could feel as good a fit as they did.

She sat for a few minutes. He could hear her deep breaths. He didn't want to push her any more. He knew how he would have reacted if someone had tried to push him too hard a few years ago.

She needed to be ready. She needed to be sure.

She lifted her eyes and they took on a determined edge. This was the Callie Turner who'd swept into his E.R. and told him she was in charge. This was the Callie Turner who'd made the decision to start vaccinating. This was the Callie Turner who hadn't blinked an eye at him watching her change her clothing. "I want more than one wish."

He felt relief wash over him. "Cheat. I'll give you two." His heart was thudding in his chest. He could only hope where this might go. "The first for work, the second for life." He felt his lips turning upwards, praying he wasn't reading her wrong.

She sucked in a breath and held it for a few seconds.

"The first for work," she repeated.

He nodded.

"I want to leave the DPA." As she said the words her shoulders immediately relaxed. It was almost as if someone had released the pressure in her and it had escaped. "I want to leave the DPA." She repeated the words again, this time more determinedly, with a smile starting to form on her lips.

The smile progressed, reaching across her face until her eyes started to light up. "I want to retrain. I want to work in family practice."

"You do?" He couldn't have picked that lottery ball if he'd tried.

She nodded. "I do." Those words sounded ominous. She met his eyes again and laughed.

"And your second wish?"

She stood up and pulled him up next to her. "This could be a difficult one."

Sawyer felt his heart plummet. "How so?"

She wrapped one arm around his waist. "I'm going to need some help while I retrain. I'm going to need some support."

He could see where this was going. "And where do you think you could get that support?"

"I'm kind of hoping I can rely on a friend."

"A friend?" His voice rose.

She stood on tiptoe and murmured in his ear. "It would have to be a special kind of friend. One who doesn't mind helping me study." She dropped a little kiss on his ear. "One who could make dinner and tidy up after himself because I'm going to be really busy."

He nodded. "Really busy. And where do you think you could find someone to meet all these demands?"

She ran her fingers down his chest. "I'm kind of hoping my genie can arrange it."

"Oh, you are?" He pulled her closer. She molded her body to his and wrapped her arms around his neck.

He got a waft of her raspberry shampoo. This was

going to drive him crazy. Hopefully for the next fifty years.

She pulled back a little. "Come to think of it, most genies grant three wishes. I guess mine kind of short-changed me."

"Why, what would be your third wish?"

She stood on tiptoe again and whispered in his ear, with a sparkle in her eyes and a pink tinge to her cheeks.

"Now, that I *can* make happen straight away."

And he took her by the hand and led her down the corridor.

EPILOGUE

IT WAS A perfect day.

The deep blue water was lapping up onto Osterman beach. Callie wiggled her feet and felt the sand shift under her toes. The ocean breeze blew her hair around her face, one side catching more of the breeze than the other. She grabbed a few strands and tucked them behind her ear.

The white canopy above her swayed in the wind, shading the guests from the early morning sun. She sighed and relaxed back into her white canvas chair and closed her eyes.

There hadn't been time for much sleep last night. Sawyer had just arrived back from his latest conference for the DPA and had been anxious to show her how much he had missed her. His new role as a DPA lecturer had been a surprise for them both. But he'd embraced it with more enthusiasm and vigor than he'd apparently possessed in years.

She could hear the ripple of voices around her. The ceremony was due to start in few minutes. There was a thud as Sawyer flopped into the chair next to her.

"How are you doing, beautiful?" He leaned over and dropped a kiss on her lips. She caught a whiff of his aftershave and touched his newly bare jaw.

"You've shaved. I was kind of liking the jungle warrior look." His hair was still slightly damp from his shower and she pushed it back from his eyes. "Next thing, you'll be having a haircut. Then I *really* won't recognize you."

He gave her a cheeky smile. "Never gonna happen."

She kept her hand on his face as she ran her eyes up and down his body. He was wearing a pale blue shirt with the sleeves rolled up and white cotton chinos. She stared down at his feet, at his toes pushing the sand around like her own.

"What happened to the shoes I bought you?"

He let out a laugh. "I decided to go native." He held out his hands at the beautiful scenery, "Somehow I don't think anyone will notice."

His phone buzzed and he pulled it from his pocket, a smile instantly appearing on his face. He handed the phone over. It was a text message with a photo of Jack and Ben, complete with Stetsons, on vacation in Texas. Jill had added the words *With thanks to you both. xx.* Jack still looked a little frail and both boys still had pockmarks on their arms.

Callie sighed. "They look so much happier. I'm so glad they're doing well."

The music started and they both stood, turning to watch Alison, her husband and three kids walk down the sandy aisle between the chairs. Jonas, her eight-month-old, was held in her arms. He was wearing a white and blue sailor suit and hat and was chewing on his thumb.

He was older than the average baby who was christened, but Alison had wanted to wait until she could arrange something special. This was truly a baby to celebrate.

Callie felt a surge of warmth in her chest. He was the picture of health. It had been great relief to everyone that Alison had never shown any symptoms of monkeypox.

"Can we have the godparents, please?"

She felt a sharp nudge as Sawyer stood and held out his hand towards her. "Shall we?"

She slid her hand into his. It still gave her the same little tingle along her spine that it had all those months ago when they'd met.

Time had flown past. She'd handed in her resignation to the DPA and had started to retrain for family practice. From the first day and hour that she'd started, she'd known she'd made the right decision.

Family practice was so much broader than any other specialty. She got to see a little of everything and she loved it—from young people to old, from runny noses to lumps and bumps. More than anything she got to spend more time with her patients and follow through on their care. It was a better fit than she could ever have imagined.

She smiled and straightened her flowery summer dress before joining the family at the front.

The ceremony was over quickly. The family gave thanks and Jonas was officially named, with Callie and Sawyer the proud godparents.

Just when she thought it was time to head for the buffet lunch, Alison turned to face her friends and colleagues. "If you'll just give me a few more minutes." She waited for people to settle back into their seats.

She smiled at Sawyer and Callie. "Most of you will know how I met Jonas's godparents. And I'm delighted that they agreed to take the role today and join us in this beautiful location."

She paused, before giving Callie a knowing smile. "And it seems such a waste to let this be over so quickly." Then, in the blink of an eye, she sat back down.

Callie was stunned. Had she missed something? What had just happened? Was that it? Were they supposed to head off to the beautifully decorated buffet tables for lunch?

A glass was pressed into her hand, the cold condensation quickly capturing her attention. Sawyer was grinning at her. She took a quick sip. Champagne with a strawberry at the bottom. Delicious.

She watched as waiters appeared and passed glasses to all the guests. How nice. Had Sawyer arranged this to drink a toast to the baby?

He straightened up and cleared his throat. "I'm sorry for stealing Alison's thunder, but she gave me a severe talking to a few weeks ago." He gave her a little nod. "About not wasting time."

Callie felt her heart start to flutter in her chest. *No.* He couldn't be.

But he was. He'd dropped to one knee.

"Callie Turner, I've only known you for twelve months. And it's official—you drive me crazy."

The guests started to laugh.

"I've never met anyone who can burn mac n' cheese like you can. Or who can take up an entire closet with shoes."

She felt herself blush. Maybe she had gone a little overboard in making him build her a special shoes closet, particularly when she wasn't wearing any right now.

"But what I've realized in this life is that when you find someone who makes your heart sing like you do, who makes you think about everything that you do, and who you don't want to spend a day without, then you should never let them go." His pale green eyes met hers and she could see his sincerity.

"Callie, when I met you I thought I was in the wrong place at the wrong time. I couldn't believe I was so unlucky to come across an infectious disease and be stuck in the middle of it all again." He shook his head. "I didn't know how wrong I was."

"I'd been stuck in the wrong place and the wrong time for the last six years. This time—for once in my life—I was in the right place at the right time. Because it's where I met you."

The crowd gave a little sigh.

"Callie, the whole world knows that I love you. I want you to be the first thing I see every morning and the last thing I see every night. Would you do me the honour of becoming my wife?"

He'd opened a small box and a beautiful solitaire diamond glistened in the sun.

She couldn't speak. She couldn't say anything. She was too stunned.

Sawyer, the man who couldn't plan anything, had completely and utterly sideswiped her.

"I can read your mind, I know this isn't in the plan, honey, but do you think you can say something? I'm getting a cramp down here." Beads of sweat were breaking out on his forehead.

He was nervous.

For the first time since she'd known him Sawyer was nervous. It was kind of cute. But she didn't want to prolong his agony. She didn't want to panic the man she loved.

And she didn't want to give him a chance to change his mind.

She bent down and didn't hesitate. "How about a yes," she whispered.

"Yes!"

He swept his arms around her waist and swung her round.

She was laughing and he was squeezing the breath out of her with his enthusiastic grip. "Wait a minute, there's one condition."

He settled her feet back on the sand and slid the diamond ring onto her finger. "Anything, honey, you name it. Your wish is my command." He gave her a low bow.

She smiled. Plans could work both ways. "Well…" she ran her finger down his cheek "…since you made such good plans for today, I'm thinking that maybe you should be in charge of the wedding plans too."

His face dropped instantly then he tried to recover with a nervous smile. "If that's what you want, honey."

She reached up for him again and planted her lips on his. "Perfect."

* * * * *

Mills & Boon® Hardback
August 2013

ROMANCE

The Billionaire's Trophy	Lynne Graham
Prince of Secrets	Lucy Monroe
A Royal Without Rules	Caitlin Crews
A Deal with Di Capua	Cathy Williams
Imprisoned by a Vow	Annie West
Duty At What Cost?	Michelle Conder
The Rings that Bind	Michelle Smart
An Inheritance of Shame	Kate Hewitt
Faking It to Making It	Ally Blake
Girl Least Likely to Marry	Amy Andrews
The Cowboy She Couldn't Forget	Patricia Thayer
A Marriage Made in Italy	Rebecca Winters
Miracle in Bellaroo Creek	Barbara Hannay
The Courage To Say Yes	Barbara Wallace
All Bets Are On	Charlotte Phillips
Last-Minute Bridesmaid	Nina Harrington
Daring to Date Dr Celebrity	Emily Forbes
Resisting the New Doc In Town	Lucy Clark

MEDICAL

Miracle on Kaimotu Island	Marion Lennox
Always the Hero	Alison Roberts
The Maverick Doctor and Miss Prim	Scarlet Wilson
About That Night...	Scarlet Wilson

0713 GEN STD HB

Mills & Boon® Large Print

August 2013

ROMANCE

Master of her Virtue	Miranda Lee
The Cost of her Innocence	Jacqueline Baird
A Taste of the Forbidden	Carole Mortimer
Count Valieri's Prisoner	Sara Craven
The Merciless Travis Wilde	Sandra Marton
A Game with One Winner	Lynn Raye Harris
Heir to a Desert Legacy	Maisey Yates
Sparks Fly with the Billionaire	Marion Lennox
A Daddy for Her Sons	Raye Morgan
Along Came Twins…	Rebecca Winters
An Accidental Family	Ami Weaver

HISTORICAL

The Dissolute Duke	Sophia James
His Unusual Governess	Anne Herries
An Ideal Husband?	Michelle Styles
At the Highlander's Mercy	Terri Brisbin
The Rake to Redeem Her	Julia Justiss

MEDICAL

The Brooding Doc's Redemption	Kate Hardy
An Inescapable Temptation	Scarlet Wilson
Revealing The Real Dr Robinson	Dianne Drake
The Rebel and Miss Jones	Annie Claydon
The Son that Changed his Life	Jennifer Taylor
Swallowbrook's Wedding of the Year	Abigail Gordon

Mills & Boon® Hardback
September 2013

ROMANCE

Challenging Dante	Lynne Graham
Captivated by Her Innocence	Kim Lawrence
Lost to the Desert Warrior	Sarah Morgan
His Unexpected Legacy	Chantelle Shaw
Never Say No to a Caffarelli	Melanie Milburne
His Ring Is Not Enough	Maisey Yates
A Reputation to Uphold	Victoria Parker
A Whisper of Disgrace	Sharon Kendrick
If You Can't Stand the Heat...	Joss Wood
Maid of Dishonour	Heidi Rice
Bound by a Baby	Kate Hardy
In the Line of Duty	Ami Weaver
Patchwork Family in the Outback	Soraya Lane
Stranded with the Tycoon	Sophie Pembroke
The Rebound Guy	Fiona Harper
Greek for Beginners	Jackie Braun
A Child to Heal Their Hearts	Dianne Drake
Sheltered by Her Top-Notch Boss	Joanna Neil

MEDICAL

The Wife He Never Forgot	Anne Fraser
The Lone Wolf's Craving	Tina Beckett
Re-awakening His Shy Nurse	Annie Claydon
Safe in His Hands	Amy Ruttan

0813 GEN STD HB

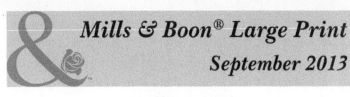

Mills & Boon® Large Print
September 2013

ROMANCE

A Rich Man's Whim	Lynne Graham
A Price Worth Paying?	Trish Morey
A Touch of Notoriety	Carole Mortimer
The Secret Casella Baby	Cathy Williams
Maid for Montero	Kim Lawrence
Captive in his Castle	Chantelle Shaw
Heir to a Dark Inheritance	Maisey Yates
Anything but Vanilla...	Liz Fielding
A Father for Her Triplets	Susan Meier
Second Chance with the Rebel	Cara Colter
First Comes Baby...	Michelle Douglas

HISTORICAL

The Greatest of Sins	Christine Merrill
Tarnished Amongst the Ton	Louise Allen
The Beauty Within	Marguerite Kaye
The Devil Claims a Wife	Helen Dickson
The Scarred Earl	Elizabeth Beacon

MEDICAL

NYC Angels: Redeeming The Playboy	Carol Marinelli
NYC Angels: Heiress's Baby Scandal	Janice Lynn
St Piran's: The Wedding!	Alison Roberts
Sydney Harbour Hospital: Evie's Bombshell	Amy Andrews
The Prince Who Charmed Her	Fiona McArthur
His Hidden American Beauty	Connie Cox

0813 GEN STD LP